Joe and Wishbone whirled around. . . .

The rusty metal door at the base of the lighthouse had banged open. Standing there with one hand on the door was a gray-haired man who glared at them.

"Get off my light!" he roared.

Wishbone yipped. Joe felt his heart banging in his chest. His first thought, which was quite a wild idea, was that a ghost had appeared. He stammered, "I-I . . . w-was ju-just tying—"

"Get back in the boat, Joe!" Rhonda called out, her voice sharp and urgent.

Joe jumped back down into the boat. Then he picked up Wishbone and helped him get aboard, too.

The old man stalked forward. "Don't come back!" he thundered. "Never come back! Doom waits for ye if ye set foot on Skeleton Reef! Doom, do ye hear? Doom, I say!"

Wishbone Mysteries

THE TREASURE OF SKELETON REEF

by Brad Strickland and Thomas E. Fuller

WISHBONE™ created by Rick Duffield

Big Red Chair Books™, *A Division of Lyrick Publishing*™

This book is a work of fiction. The characters, incidents, and dialogues are products of the author's imagination and are not to be construed as real. Any resemblance to actual events or persons, living or dead, is entirely coincidental.

 Big Red Chair Books™, *A Division of Lyrick Publishing*™
300 E. Bethany Drive, Allen, Texas 75002

©1997 Big Feats! Entertainment

Edited by Kevin Ryan

Copy edited by Jonathon Brodman

Cover concept, design, and interior illustrations by Lyle Miller

Wishbone photograph by Carol Kaelson

Library of Congress Catalog Card Number: 97-73280

ISBN: 1-57064-279-6

First printing: November 1997

10 9 8 7 6 5 4 3 2 1

Printed in the United States of America

*To Gail, Karen, and Stephen, whose adventures
in growing up I shared.*
—Brad Strickland

*To my children—Edward, Anthony, John, and
Christina—whose own adventures are just beginning.*
—Thomas E. Fuller

FROM THE BIG RED CHAIR . . .

Oh . . . hi! Wishbone here. You caught me right in the middle of some of my favorite things—books. Let me welcome you to my brand-new book series, WISHBONE MYSTERIES. In each story, I help my human friends solve a puzzling mystery. In *THE TREASURE OF SKELETON REEF*, I work with my best friend, Joe, to solve the mystery involving a spooky lighthouse and some lost pirate treasure!

This story takes place in early summer, just before the events that you'll see in the second season of my WISHBONE television show. In this story, Joe is fourteen and about to enter eighth grade. And just like me, he's always ready for adventure.

You're in for a real treat, so pull up a chair and a snack and sink your teeth into *THE TREASURE OF SKELETON REEF*!

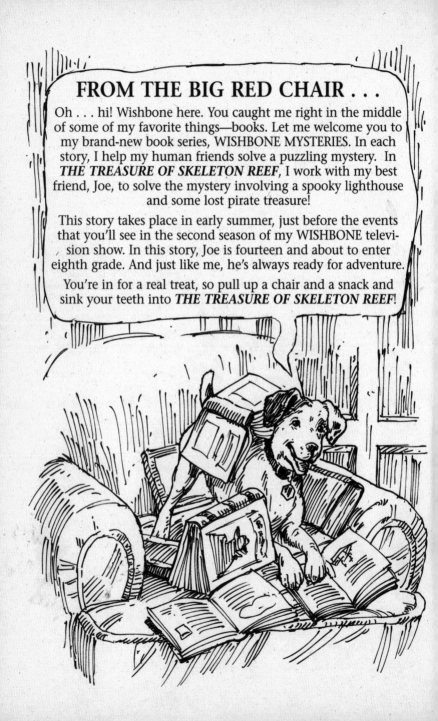

Chapter One

"Uh . . . excuse me. Is anyone there? Helllooo!" Wishbone turned this way and that, trying to peek through an air hole in his pet carrier. He had no luck. Suitcases, boxes, and other luggage blocked his view. The constant roar of the jet's engines would surely have drowned him out anyway—even if anyone *did* ever listen to the dog!

Hmm . . . I can't see a thing! Well, if the eyes can't peek, the nose can sniff! The white-with-brown-spots dog thrust his black, shiny nose against one of the air holes. Then he took a deep, deep snuffle.

"Ah, yes! Much better. Let me see . . . I can smell leather and plastic—lots of clothes—and up above me somewhere, someone is eating airline food! Oh, it's not fair at all to be impounded in the luggage compartment!" Wishbone scratched at the carrier, wishing that he had been able to fly sitting in the passengers' compartment, next to his best friend, fourteen-year-old Joe Talbot. Unfortunately, the airline had rules, and one of them was that dogs had to fly with the luggage.

That was the bad part. The luggage compartment was dark, cold, and cramped. The jet engines made it vibrate, too, sometimes so hard that Wishbone's teeth chattered. Oh, well . . . A dog who wasn't able to eat could always take a nap. Wishbone curled up inside the carrier, thought wistfully of airline food, and somehow he dozed for a long time.

He woke up with a jolt as the airplane lowered its landing gear and then touched the ground. Bump! Bump! The engines screamed, and Wishbone felt his travel carrier slipping across the floor. It jounced against a big suitcase. "Whoa! I'll bet up where the people are, the flight attendants told them to buckle their seat belts! I just slide around loose, like a backpack full of socks!"

Wishbone was far too excited to stay grumpy for long. A few minutes later the cargo hatch opened with a hiss. Wishbone smelled busy airline workers. One of them picked up his carrier and said, "Hope you had a good flight, Mr. Wishbone Talbot!" Then the worker put him down on a cart, along with everything else from the airplane's hold.

Wishbone took another deep sniff. "It wasn't bad, thanks, but I'm *really* looking forward to getting out of this thing. I mean, it's hard to have an intelligent conversation with luggage!"

Bright, hot sunlight streamed through the air holes in his pet carrier. Wishbone glimpsed the big airliner he had traveled on. The cart was attached to a small tractor-like truck, and one of the workers climbed into the seat and started the engine. The cart lurched forward, and Wishbone nearly tumbled down.

"Watch it! Valuable cargo here!"

The truck drove through a big door like an oversize garage door. Then Wishbone saw they had gone inside a huge room. He heard and smelled more airline workers all around. Then one of them picked up his

carrier. Wishbone felt himself being plunked down on something that rattled, rocked, and moved him along—a conveyor belt!

"All right! This is sort of like an amusement-park ride for suitcases—and dogs! *Whee!*"

The belt rumbled him along through a dark tunnel, then up a steep incline. At the top, light burst in again. Someone picked up the carrier, swung it to one side, and put it down. Soon the person stacked other luggage around him. Wishbone began to feel impatient again.

"Come on, people! This dog's got places to go, people to see, an airport to explore! And a little trip outside would be great, too, if you get my meaning. Oh, Joe, where are you!"

Joe Talbot, Wishbone's best friend, was standing in the baggage-claim area of the airport, anxiously looking for Wishbone. He had retrieved his suitcase, but where was the tan-plastic pet carrier? He was beginning to worry—what if there had been a mix-up? He had heard about airlines losing luggage. Joe hoped Wishbone hadn't accidentally wound up on a plane heading for some strange destination like Timbuktu or Kalamazoo. Then, as Joe looked through a stack of suitcases, he heard a bark and laughed in relief. "Hey, there you are! Over behind the trunk!"

Wishbone yipped again. Joe picked up the carrier easily. He played basketball, and he was in good physical shape.

"I'll bet you want to get out and run around, don't you, boy?" He hefted his suitcase in one hand, and Wishbone's travel case in the other.

Joe felt great. The airplane trip had been fun, and he had the best kind of seat—right by the window. He had watched the airport shrink away, and until the airplane had climbed up into the clouds, he had enjoyed the view. Then he had read a good book for most of the trip, before the plane came out of the clouds above a sunny landscape of green fields, ribbon-like highways, and, off in the distance, the Gulf of Mexico.

Now Joe walked excitedly through the airport, eager to get on with his vacation. He passed the ticket counter. Ahead, through a glass door, he could see his mom, Ellen Talbot, and their next-door neighbor, Wanda Gilmore, standing on the curb in the bright sunshine. The automatic door hissed open as Joe headed outside.

"There he is," Ellen said to Wanda. She had her one large suitcase at her feet. She was dressed for hot weather in a flower-print blouse, light-colored slacks,

10

and dark sunglasses. Wanda wore somewhat more colorful clothes and a big, floppy-brimmed hat, besides.

Joe felt Wishbone shifting around inside the carrier as he stepped into the hot sunshine. "I think Wishbone wants out of the carrier, Mom. Do you think it would be all right to let him out now? He's been stuck in this cage for a long time."

Ellen smiled and nodded. "I think so, Joe. Put his leash on, though."

Joe set the pet carrier down with a thump and opened the door. "Come on, boy. It's a lot brighter than it was back in Oakdale—and a whole lot hotter!"

Wishbone leaped out into dazzling sunlight, blinking and grinning. Joe clipped the leash to Wishbone's collar. Wishbone's brown-haired best friend wore a loose red polo shirt, baggy blue shorts, and white socks and sneakers. He ruffled Wishbone's ears.

"Better, boy?" Joe said.

Wishbone strained at his leash, looking eager to explore the new territory.

"Look, Joe," said Wanda Gilmore, pointing. Wanda was a thin, sharp-featured, auburn-haired woman who nowadays complained about Wishbone only when he dug up her flowerbeds. She was gesturing toward a corner of the parking lot. Joe could see a square of green grass, planted with flowers, brushy bushes, and strange-looking trees. "The sign says that's a pet rest room. Maybe you'd better see if Wishbone wants to visit it."

Wishbone immediately tugged at the leash. Joe led him over to the square—or, rather, he followed his eager pet. Soon the Jack Russell terrier was sniffing the flowers, strange bushes, and trees. "You've never seen a palm tree before, have you, fella?" Joe asked, amused at Wishbone's excitement.

11

Maybe Wishbone hadn't, but he immediately showed that he knew what a tree was for, no matter what kind it was.

Joe wiped his hand over his perspiring forehead and puffed out his cheeks. "I know one thing, boy. You're going to be hot in that fur coat. St. George Bay may be a great beach town, but it's broiling-hot here."

Wishbone opened his mouth, rolled out his long pink tongue, and panted happily.

Joe grinned, glad to see that Wishbone had a way to beat the heat. He turned and shaded his eyes as he looked around. "I wonder where the beach is." Something popped out of his back pocket and fell softly to the sandy ground.

Before Joe could stoop to retrieve it, Wishbone ran over and picked up the paperback book Joe had dropped. With his mouth full, he pawed at Joe's leg for attention.

Joe grinned. "Thanks, Wishbone." He took the book from Wishbone's mouth. "I bought this to read on the airplane." Joe studied the cover of the paperback. "*Sherlock Holmes: His Greatest Cases.* I finished about six of the stories." He had been stumped by the mysteries—and impressed when the great, pipe-puffing British detective Sherlock Holmes solved the cases. With a twitch of the leash, Joe said, "Ready to go back, boy? Ms. Gilmore's cousin is supposed to pick us up any time now."

Wishbone trotted beside Joe, head high, eyes alert. He and Joe passed a little bright green lizard that scurried under a bush. A jet roared by overhead, making the pair look up into the clear blue sky. A bright red-yellow-and-black butterfly fluttered by, and Joe had to hold on hard to the leash to keep Wishbone from starting a game of tag with it.

Wanda was fanning herself with her airline-ticket holder. "I wonder what's keeping Rhonda," she said, looking out across the airport parking lot.

Ellen sounded amused. "Maybe it's because we made such good time, Wanda. Our plane landed fifteen minutes early."

"Well, *I* would have driven to the airport early if she were coming to visit me," Wanda responded. She sighed. "What are you reading, Joe?"

Joe showed her the book. "It's a collection of Sherlock Holmes stories. I read almost half of them on the plane."

"Your dad always loved mystery stories," Ellen said.

Joe's dad had died when Joe was only six. Sometimes Joe really missed him. He looked at the cover of his paperback, which showed Sherlock Holmes and his crime-fighting partner, Dr. Watson, walking down a foggy London street. Thinking of his father, Joe said, "I wonder if he ever read this one."

"Oh, I'm sure he did," Wanda replied. "After all, Sherlock Holmes is a classic. Do you like the stories?"

Joe shrugged and smiled. "It's a lot of fun to try to figure out the mysteries before Sherlock Holmes does. It's hard, too—he's a lot sharper than most people. I feel more like Dr. Watson than I do like Holmes, because Dr. Watson is always about a step and a half behind."

Ellen laughed. "Look at Wishbone! He almost looks as if he enjoys the Sherlock Holmes stories, too."

Joe looked down and chuckled at the way Wishbone was thumping his tail. Sometimes, Joe thought, Wishbone really looked as if he understood everything that was going on around him.

"There she is!" Wanda shouted. "Over here, Rhonda!"

Joe looked up and blinked. "Wow! Look at that car! I didn't know your cousin was rich." An old-fashioned car with a long, long hood and a beautifully polished silvery radiator was rolling steadily toward them. The car was burgundy, and its finish glistened in the hot sun. A rear side window was down, and a blue-sleeved arm waved at them.

"It's a Rolls-Royce!" Ellen sounded very impressed. "Wanda, you should have told us!"

"Oh, Rhonda's just family," Wanda said. "She inherited a pile of money, but she's very down to earth. Besides, there's some kind of trust fund she has inherited that keeps her on an allowance. Even though she has a great house and car, she's not really like a rich person. And she's very friendly. The minute I called her and told her about our trip to see the Skeleton Reef Lighthouse, she insisted that we stay with her." She waved at the approaching car and called, "Hi, Rhonda!"

The big car whispered to a smooth stop at the curb. The back door flew open, and—Joe blinked—a woman who looked a little like Wanda bounded out. She had the same auburn hair (a little longer, though) and similar sharp features. However, Wanda was thin and about average height. Rhonda was a head taller; she looked heavier and more muscular in her blue jogging suit. She threw her arms around Wanda and said, "I'm so glad to see you! My favorite cousin!"

"Well, thank you!" Wanda was laughing. "Cousin Rhonda, this is my good friend and next-door neighbor, Ellen Talbot. And this is Ellen's son, Joe, and Joe's best friend, Wishbone."

Rhonda shook hands with Ellen and Joe. Then she knelt and held her hand out. Wishbone sniffed it and then lifted his front paw politely. Laughing,

Rhonda shook it. "Welcome, everyone! Now, I know my cousin dragged you here because of that silly lighthouse, but I want you to enjoy your visit. So are you ready to do a little sight-seeing?"

"Sure," Ellen said. "We've never been to the Gulf of Mexico before."

"Oh, you're going to see that—and lots more," promised Rhonda. She turned toward the car. A trim, elderly man had climbed out from the driver's seat. He wore a neat khaki uniform. "Carperdale, help our guests load their luggage."

"Yes, madam." Joe could not help staring. Carperdale sounded British. He was thin, with twinkling eyes and a brushy white moustache. *Just like in the movies*, Joe thought. Then something else struck him: *He looks a lot like Dr. Watson in the Sherlock Holmes stories!*

As Carperdale was putting the suitcases in the enormous trunk of the Rolls, Joe asked Rhonda, "You have a chauffeur?"

Rhonda laughed. "Oh, Carperdale worked for my late Uncle Hugo for thirty years. When Uncle Hugo passed away ten years ago, he left Carperdale a pension. I expected him to move back to England, but he said, 'If I should do that, madam, who would take care of the automobile and the house?' So he's not exactly a chauffeur. He's more of a caretaker, I guess—for the house, the car, and even me!"

"I'm looking forward to this," Wanda said as Carperdale shut the trunk gently. "I've never ridden in a Rolls-Royce before."

Rhonda laughed. "And you're not riding in one this time, either, silly. I've arranged for bikes."

"Bikes?" asked Ellen, sounding uncertain.

"Bikes!" answered Rhonda. "Tandem bikes, also known as bicycles built for two! Wonderful for the heart and lungs! Best way of traveling known to man or beast." She looked down. "No offense, Wishbone."

Wishbone grinned up at her as if to say, "None taken, Rhonda!"

Wanda looked doubtfully at the tandem bikes. "I'm not sure about this."

On the other hand, Joe couldn't wait to try this new type of bike. He felt excited as they followed Rhonda to where the bikes waited in a side lot of the airport. One was bright red, the other deep blue, and two bike helmets hung on the handlebar of each one.

The blue bike had a very deep basket—big enough for Wishbone to sit in comfortably—so Joe and Ellen took that one. Joe was on the lead seat. After a wobbly trial run, he and Ellen found they could get around pretty well. Joe carefully put Wishbone into the basket and cautioned, "Now stay put, boy."

Wanda climbed onto the red bike behind Rhonda. Then they were off, pedaling away from the airport. The burgundy Rolls-Royce followed along at only about ten miles per hour.

"Look!" Rhonda said as they turned onto a long, straight bike path that ran beside an asphalt highway. Huge old trees shaded the riders. Gray-green Spanish moss, like long, tangled beards, trailed down from the tree branches. On the other side of the highway, through breaks in the trees, a deep blue gleam of water revealed itself. "There's the Gulf!"

Joe grinned. School was all right, but it had lasted for nine solid months. Now, the first week of summer break, he was off to a whole exciting new place. "Come on, let's go a little faster," he said to his companions.

Ellen laughed. "I'm game if you are!" They bent

16

forward and made the bike speed along. Joe enjoyed the breeze and the glimpses of the Gulf.

In the basket, Wishbone had his tongue lolling. Joe thought his canine friend was enjoying the trip. After a long airplane ride in the luggage compartment, he was probably ready for a little freedom. Joe was feeling up for some excitement, too.

"Where's the lighthouse?" Wanda said, panting, as she and Rhonda pedaled along beside Joe and Ellen.

For a moment Rhonda didn't answer. Then she said, "Well, cousin, there's bad news about that, but don't worry about it right now. Just enjoy the ride."

"Bad news?" Wanda asked.

"Come on," Rhonda said to Joe and Ellen. "Race you to the corner of the city park!"

Joe had wondered what the bad news might be, but with Rhonda grinning at him, he started to pump the pedals. The bikes rushed along. Under the heat of the sun, with the sea breeze in his face, Joe forgot for a moment about everything but winning the race. In the basket, Wishbone leaned forward, his eager nose twitching.

It was beginning to look like a great vacation, Joe decided.

Chapter Two

"Tell me all about how you got mixed up with the lighthouse," Rhonda said. The race had ended in a draw—though Joe suspected that Rhonda had not pedaled as hard as she might have. At a slower speed, the two bikes rolled past tall palm trees, blue and pink beach houses, and small brick stores. Joe, still getting his wind back from the race, listened to what the cousins were saying. Wanda had enjoyed being mysterious about the reason for their trip. Now he wanted to learn exactly what it was all about.

"Well," Wanda said, still a little out of breath, "it was a chance too good to pass up. Last week I got a call from the Windom Foundation lawyer. Do you know about the Windom family, Rhonda?"

Rhonda laughed. "Of course I do! Before they went west to help build Oakdale, the Windoms lived right here in St. George Bay. They used to be a rich family."

As the bike trail narrowed, Joe, Ellen, and Wishbone dropped back and followed behind Wanda and Rhonda. They had come to the downtown section of St. George Bay, with colorful shops on both sides of the wide street. Wishbone sniffed.

19

Joe chuckled. "I think you're going to enjoy St. George Bay, boy! I see a pizza shop, a hamburger restaurant, and a hot-dog stand. I'll bet this is more fun than sticking your head out the car window."

Wishbone's tongue lolled as if he agreed.

Joe heard Wanda, still gasping for air, say, "Right. Well, the Windoms owned the Skeleton Reef Light here in St. George Bay. It's very, very old—it dates all the way back to the 1700s. The lawyer said that the Windom Foundation wanted to give the lighthouse to some deserving non-profit group, and he knew I was president of the Oakdale Historical Society. It was odd, but there seemed to be some rush. So he was wondering if the historical society could take immediate possession of the lighthouse. Of course, I agreed at once!"

Rhonda sounded cautious. "Did the lawyer tell you about the work that's needed?"

"Oh, he said the lighthouse needed some fixing up. That's why I talked Ellen and Joe into coming along with me. It's a vacation for them, and they can help me tidy and dust when they're not enjoying the beach."

With a snort, Rhonda said, "Tidy and dust! Cousin, you don't know what you've gotten yourself into!"

Her tone made Joe feel a little uneasy. From her seat behind him, Ellen called, "What do you mean?"

"Oh, you'll see soon enough," Rhonda assured her, looking back over her shoulder. "Now follow me. It's only another mile or so!"

"This part of town looks old," Joe said as they cycled past two antique brick warehouses with faded signs painted on them. One was the Gulf-Fresh Oyster Company, and the other was the Bay Shrimpery. Joe thought that neither warehouse looked as if it had been used in about half a century.

Rhonda nodded back at him. "It *is* old, Joe. St. George Bay is one of the oldest seaports on the Gulf. It was part of the Spanish colonial empire in the late 1600s. Then later on it became an English-occupied town. Why, back in the 1750s, it was a pirate hideout!"

Joe said, "Hey, settle down, Wishbone!" The Jack Russell terrier had jumped, almost as if he were excited to hear about pirates. Joe thought about the great pirate tales he knew—stories of Blackbeard, Long John Silver, and all the rest. He decided he and Wishbone might spend some time investigating St. George Bay's pirate-inhabited past.

The group pedaled all the way through town, past sleepy old parks shaded by moss-draped oaks, past more old brick warehouses, past strolling crowds of friendly people who waved at them. Even though Joe was used to exercising, he began to feel tired. His legs strained to pedal the bike. Ahead of him, Wanda was huffing and puffing. Then they turned toward the Gulf of Mexico. Joe could see its water shimmering through the trees ahead.

Just before they got close enough to view the beach, Rhonda turned the red bike in at a long, curving driveway that led between two rows of palm trees. "Here we are!"

Joe grinned. "Cool!" The house where Rhonda lived was three stories tall, and it had wide, screened-in porches running all around it. An octagonal tower at one side rose two stories higher than the rest of the house. Thick beds of sharp-leafed palmettos and aloe grew in the front yard. They looked like bunches of light green swords jutting out in all directions. A sandy space next to the garage served as a parking lot for two yellow-and-black trucks. The scent of fresh paint came from the house.

21

Rhonda and Wanda rode their bike up to the front steps, and Rhonda hopped off first. "You'll have to excuse the workmen," Rhonda said. "My great-great-uncle, Cuthbert Gilmore, built this place. The local folks used to call it Gilmore's Folly. We call it Gilmore's Rest. Anyway, fixing it up is *my* little restoration project. Come this way."

Joe and Ellen parked their bike, and Joe helped Wishbone down from his basket. They followed Rhonda around to the side of the house. "Oh!" Ellen said with a gasp. "What a lovely view!"

Joe agreed. "Terrific!"

The house overlooked St. George Bay. A few hundred yards away, a white, sandy beach glistened in the sun. The blue water sparkled. Joe could see sailboats leaning gracefully away from the wind, their red and white and yellow sails looking like shining triangles.

Rising from the water in the open bay was an old tower. Its bricks were grayish-white. It had a half-moon window about halfway up. Above that was a smaller, round window. A glassed-in story that housed the lamp chamber was near the top of the lighthouse. Above that was the rusty-red cone-shaped roof. "The Skeleton Reef Light!" Wanda said, sounding thrilled.

"Yes," her cousin replied in a dry voice. "That, I believe, is *your* restoration project, cousin—if you can get it finished by September 1, that is."

"It looks as if it's just sitting right in the water," Joe observed, wondering how it had been constructed that way.

Rhonda nodded. "It looks that way, but there's a concrete base under it. The lighthouse sits on a reef made up of oyster shells, Joe. The reef used to be bigger, but over the years hurricanes have worn it down. The tide is in right now, too, so you can't see much of the base or the reef it's built on. It's there, though—a long, low ridge that goes halfway across the bay. In the old days, a ship could run right up on that rocky ridge and tear out its bottom. Every year, four or five wooden ships would crash on the oyster reef. Their hulls would rot away. The ship timbers looked like ribs, and so the local people began calling the sandbar Skeleton Reef. The lighthouse that was built to guide ships safely around it became known as Skeleton Reef Light."

"I can't wait to get out there," Wanda said. "I want to begin fixing it up right away."

"You might get a few volunteers from town to help you," Rhonda told her. "There's a group called the St. George Lighthouse Preservation Society that might help. Still, you'll have a very, very hard job getting everything ready by the beginning of September."

23

"Why September?" Ellen asked.

Rhonda shook her head. "That lawyer didn't tell you about the deadline, did he?"

Wanda gave her cousin a sharp look. "Deadline?"

"I didn't think so. Oh, cousin, the lighthouse needs more than a coat of paint and tidying. It's falling apart! The city is going to force the owners to tear it down if it's not completely renovated by September 1."

With a surprised blink, Wanda said, "But *we're* the owners now! The Oakdale Historical Society, I mean! I signed the papers last week."

"I'm sorry," Rhonda told her. "It's going to cost you about $250,000 to repair that place. If you decide to tear it down, it will cost a bit less."

Wanda's eyes grew wide. "Oh, no! The historical society doesn't have that kind of money! An expense like that would bankrupt us!"

"Come on," Rhonda said. "Let's go inside. Maybe we can come up with some way of helping."

Carperdale had parked the big Rolls-Royce in the garage. Joe helped him unload the car while Wishbone supervised. "Thank you, Master Joseph," Carperdale said.

That form of address made Joe feel awkward. "Uh, could you just call me plain old Joe?" he asked.

Carperdale's eyes sparkled. He brushed the curling tips of his white moustache. "No, I'm afraid not, Master Joseph. Might we compromise and use 'Joseph'?"

"I suppose so."

"Excellent. I shall call your splendid little animal 'Wishbone.' And you may call me 'Carperdale.' Now, I must get these things inside, show you to your rooms, change clothes, and supervise the painting. Mr. Hugo always trusted me to oversee the painting and general maintenance."

Wishbone felt very pleased by the room he and Joe would share. It was on the second floor. He jumped up onto the bed. As he looked out the window, his tail began to wag. "Great view, Joe! We can see the bay and the lighthouse from here. I can't wait to sniff out some pirate history!"

As soon as Joe had put his suitcase and Wishbone's pet carrier away without unpacking, the two made their way to the parlor downstairs. Even before they got there, Wishbone's keen ears picked up worried voices.

Rhonda, Ellen, and Wanda were sitting on the sofa there. Wanda looked close to tears. "What am I going to do?" she murmured.

Rhonda patted her shoulder. "I don't know, dear. The Lighthouse Preservation Society doesn't have that kind of money either. I wish I could help more, but I'm on an allowance that just lets me pay the upkeep and the taxes on this place. Maybe we can think of something, though."

Joe paused in the doorway, and Wishbone sat close to his feet, looking around. The parlor was a cluttered room, with frilly lamps, a long sofa, lots of soft-looking easy chairs, scattered tables, and a whole wall of bookshelves. Wishbone approved. "Nice place, Rhonda. Lots of places for a dog of just the right size to curl up and snooze."

Ellen gave her son a smile. "Did you unpack?"

"Uh . . . no. I'll do it later," Joe said. "Wishbone and I just wondered if we could explore the house."

Rhonda smiled at him. "Oh, sure. Just don't get in the workmen's way. They're all on the second floor, I think. Otherwise, make yourself at home! You might like to start by climbing up to the top of the tower. There's a spiral staircase in the hall that leads up there. Uncle Hugo used to climb up there to watch his oyster boats sail in and out of the bay."

"Thanks. Come on, Wishbone!"

"Right behind you, Joe! Lead on!"

They found the spiral staircase, and Joe began to climb. Wishbone charged ahead of him, loving the feeling of running up the spiral stairs.

"Whoa! This is great, Joe! Just like I'm chasing my tail! Come on, Joe! Up, up, up!"

The stairs went around and around, up and up. With Wishbone leading the way, Joe climbed to the very top. He opened a creaking door, and he and Wishbone came out into a dusty room. A few old trunks stood around. Joe went to a window and gazed out. "You can see the whole town from here," he said.

Wishbone was a little too short to see the whole town, or anything else. He sniffed at the trunks and boxes instead. "Hmm . . . Obviously this room is an attic. I wonder what Sherlock Holmes would make of all this. He was a great detective—so smart he was practically canine." Wishbone sneezed. "Well, he might say Rhonda hardly ever tidies up here! That's an elementary deduction, as Holmes would call it. Now, what is this?"

Wishbone put his front feet up on a trunk and sniffed at a battered cardboard box sitting on top of it. It seemed to hold old papers. He tugged at it, and it teetered on the edge of the trunk.

"Oops! I didn't mean to knock it—yipes!"

The box toppled off the trunk, and it burst open with a *pop!* Joe turned around. "What was that? What are you doing, boy?"

26

Trying to look innocent, Wishbone gazed up at Joe. "Me? Nothing! Uh . . . it was falling off when I found it! Uh . . . did you feel that earthquake, Joe? Just a minor one, but it made the box fall right off—"

Joe shook his head. "Here, let me pick these up."

"Okay! I'd help you, but I don't have any thumbs."

Joe knelt and began to repack the box. When it had split open, a couple of dozen faded notebooks had fallen out. "These are very old," Joe said, holding one up. "This one is dated 1922."

Wishbone sniffed it. "That's almost ancient history in dog years!"

Joe opened the notebook. "Hmm . . . It belonged to Hugo J. Gilmore, Junior. This looks like a story of some kind."

Wishbone put his paw on Joe's leg. "Read it, Joe!"

Frowning at the handwriting, which had faded to a pale brown, Joe slowly began to read out loud. "'How I found the secret of the Treasure of Skeleton Reef, by Hugo Gilmore, Junior.'" Joe looked at Wishbone. "Did you hear that, boy? A treasure! Maybe pirate treasure!"

"Read on, Joe! Read on!"

Joe turned a brittle page. "'It all began when the old jail was being torn down. My father had bought the property. I was there one day, and my father showed me the cell where the pirate Black Ben Walker had been held. The bed was just three wooden planks mortared into the wall. While exploring, I looked at the underside of the bed. No one had done that for two hundred years! There, carved in the wood, I found the poem that is the key to the treasure!'"

Wishbone leaped from side to side in his excitement. "Pirate treasure! *Treasure Island! The Pirates of Penzance!* An adventure already!"

27

Joe turned the page and blinked. Then he slowly read aloud a few lines of a poem:

> "'Twas a dark, stormy night when we came to
>   grief
> And wrecked the poor Mary upon Skeleton
>   Reef—
> Stormy the sky, and dark was the night—
> Devil take the keeper o' the Skeleton Reef
>   Light!"

"There's more!" Joe told Wishbone. "There are numbers, and here's a line about golden treasure! Wishbone, let's go tell everybody what we found!"

"I'm with you, Joe! Coming through! Clear the way! Ya-ha!" Wishbone sped through the doorway and ran down the circular stairs, with Joe close behind him. At the bottom, they rushed through a doorway, and—*oof!*—Joe ran right into a girl who was carrying a tray piled high with paper-wrapped hamburgers.

The girl staggered to keep her balance, and one of the hamburgers flew off the tray and plopped onto the floor. She glared at Joe. "Watch it!"

Joe had dropped the notebook. Wishbone noticed that, but he was more interested in what the girl had dropped—it smelled like great food. Joe said, "Uh . . . sorry! Who are you?"

Wishbone glanced up. The girl looked part Asian, with black hair and dark brown eyes. She was wearing blue jeans cut off to make shorts, and a yellow T-shirt with a picture of a luscious hamburger on the front. She also wore a red baseball cap, and her black hair was pulled in a ponytail through the opening above the back strap of the cap.

"My name's Christy," she said. "Christy Lee. . . . Oh, no! Your dog!"

After his glance at her, Wishbone had nosed the fallen hamburger into a corner. He had managed to slip it out of its paper wrapper. Now, tail wagging, he was munching one of the best burgers he had ever tasted. "Yum! Free samples, Joe!"

Joe groaned. "Wishbone!"

Wishbone looked around, his mouth full. "Wha'? Didn't you see her feed the dog?"

Joe felt inside the pockets of his baggy shorts. He pulled out the paperback book, and then his wallet. "I'm sorry. Let me pay you."

"It's okay," Christy said. "Wait here, and I'll be back in a minute." She hurried up a different staircase.

Wishbone finished the last morsels of hamburger. "Great burger, Joe! Food and pirate treasure—I'm satisfied with the vacation so far!"

Worrying about what Rhonda might think, Joe picked up the hamburger paper and wiped the floor carefully, though Wishbone had not even left a crumb. A moment later, Christy came back downstairs. "I have to pick up one more burger for a painter," she said. "Come along and see my dad's restaurant. It's parked outside."

"Parked?" Joe asked. He followed Christy outside across the screened-in porch. In the sandy spot, a recreational vehicle was parked. It was painted bright red. On one side was a big sign with a hamburger just like the one on Christy's T-shirt. Under that, the sign said: FOR A SNACK ATTACK, TRY LEE'S LUNCH! Joe could smell the tempting scent of food cooking. "That's your dad's?" he asked.

29

"Yes," Christy said. "We have a restaurant in town, too, but Mom takes care of that. Meanwhile, Dad drives this lunch wagon around to construction sites—and to houses where workmen are busy." She led Joe and Wishbone around to the side of the RV. A window was propped open there. Inside was a cheerful, chubby, dark-haired man who looked Asian. "Dad," Christy said, "I need one more hamburger with everything on it."

"Coming right up!" The man turned and got busy at a grill. The hiss of a sizzling hamburger patty and the delicious aroma made Joe's mouth water. Beside him, Wishbone practically danced as he took sniff after sniff. "Who are your friends?" Christy's dad asked.

"Oh, I just ran into them," Christy said, with a grin at Joe.

"I'm Joe Talbot," Joe said. "I'm visiting Miss Gilmore with my mom and our next-door neighbor. I kind of knocked a hamburger out of Christy's tray, and my dog ate it. I'm sorry."

"Oh?" Mr. Lee turned away from the grill, leaned over the side of the RV, and looked down at Wishbone. "Did he like it?"

Wishbone panted happily. Looking down at his pleased expression, Joe said, "I'm sure he did."

Mr. Lee laughed. "Then there's nothing to be sorry about! He knows where to find the best burger in town. The secret's in the soy!" He winked. "One free hamburger as a sample. I know you'll want to buy more later on." He returned to the grill.

"Why were you running like that, anyway?" Christy asked Joe.

Joe grinned. "I just found something exciting. See this notebook? Everything in it was written back in 1922! It has a poem in it that tells where to find a pirate treasure—"

To Joe's surprise, Christy laughed. "Is that the one that starts with ''Twas a dark, stormy night'? It's the one Hugo Gilmore 'found,' right?"

"Uh . . . right," Joe said. He was puzzled at how Christy had picked up on that so fast—as quickly as Sherlock Holmes, he thought.

"Come with me," Christy said. She took them back to a door that led into the RV. The room inside was set up like a very small souvenir store. Racks held sunscreen, sunglasses, and postcards. Christy reached up and took down a shiny printed sheet. "Is the poem like this?" she asked, handing it to Joe.

The sheet was headed "The Legend of Ben Walker's Treasure." Under the title was a paragraph explaining that Hugo Gilmore, Jr., had found the poem in the old jail back in 1922. The verse itself followed, a whole page long. There were colorful sketches around the poem's border showing a ship wrecking itself on a reef, and a scowling pirate with long black hair and a tangled black beard. The poem was exactly the same as the one in the notebook.

"You mean everyone knows?" Joe asked, handing the poem back to Christy.

She shrugged. "Well, everyone in St. George Bay, anyway. It's an old legend."

Joe felt his heart sink a little. "Then someone's already found the treasure?"

Christy smiled and shook her head. "Nope. Because there's no treasure to find. Sorry, Joe. It's really just a story."

At that moment, Mr. Lee called out that the hamburger was ready. As Christy took it inside the house, Joe looked down at Wishbone. "Well," he said with a sigh, "we *almost* had an adventure, boy!"

Wishbone wasn't looking at him. Instead, he was

THE LEGEND OF BEN WALKER'S TREASURE

This poem was discovered by Hugo Gilmore, Jr. in 1922 in the St. George City Jail.

"MAD MARY'S LAMENT"
BY CAPT. BENJAMIN WALKER

'Twas a dark, stormy night when we came to grief
And wrecked the poor Mary upon Skeleton Reef—
    Stormy the sky, and dark was the night—
    Devil take the keeper o' the Skeleton Reef Light!

Golden treasure may be below
If ye drop by two-and-twenty,
The secret's there for ye to know,
    And gold be there in plenty!
Faith's a friend, and there begin,
And bear five points to starboard.
Pull hearty then, and pull to win,
    Pull with all your might—
And with each pull, may my curse fall,
    Devil take the keeper o' the Skeleton Reef Light!

Bear down ten, bear another five,
Hope for luck, and three and thirty;
Then larboard, seven and twenty strive.
    'Tis gold, 'tis gold, ye seek for charity,
Three Sisters will guard it there for ye.
Seek when the moon be shining bright,
And Devil take the keeper o' the Skeleton Reef Light!

Now may ye fare better than the Mad Mary,
    The craft that was so dear to me,
    Swift as a bird in her sea-flight,
    Ne'er again will her guns fight,
    Ne'er again will she please my sight,
Oh, Devil take the keeper o' the
    Skeleton Reef Light!

sniffing the air suspiciously, the fur on his neck bristling.

Puzzled, Joe said, "What's wrong, boy?"

At that moment, something orange moved in the driver's seat of the RV. Through the open window leaped the largest, shaggiest cat Joe had ever seen.

Chapter Three

Wishbone growled, feeling his muscles tense. "Stay away from Joe, you big orange monster!"

"Wow!" Joe said. "That is one huge cat!"

From the lunch-counter section of the RV, Mr. Lee peered around. "Oh, that's Cap'n Ahab. He belongs to Christy, or vice versa, I sometimes think."

Wishbone stared. "Uh . . . excuse me, but I think the whale's name was Moby Dick! Only I doubt if the whale was as big as that!"

Cap'n Ahab was a shaggy orange tom with darker orange stripes. His right ear was torn, as if he'd been in a fight sometime in the past. Over his right eye he wore a black eye patch, and his left eye glared at the world with a yellow, cunning stare. He looked at Wishbone, sat down, and began to lick himself.

Wishbone growled again. Joe reached down and hooked a finger around his collar. "No, boy!"

Just then Christy returned, running down the front steps. She laughed when she saw Joe holding Wishbone back. "Don't worry about Cap'n Ahab. Every dog in town is afraid of him."

Wishbone strained, wanting to chase away the beast. "Though I'm not scared of any cat, I can see why! He must weigh forty pounds!"

"Could I buy a hamburger?" Joe asked. "That seems only fair."

"Sure," Christy said. "Dad, one burger for Joe," Christy called to her father. Then she turned around to face Joe. "How do you like your burger? With everything?"

"I don't know," Joe confessed. "What does 'everything' mean?"

In a singsong voice, Christy said, "A luscious quarter-pound patty on a special seeded bun tastes really great with Monterey Jack cheese, lettuce, tomato, onions, and Lee's Special Sauce. If you want jalapeños, black olives, bacon, mushrooms, or Cheddar cheese, we'll add them in a flash, for just a bit more cash!"

Joe laughed. "I guess I'll have it just with the cheese, lettuce, tomato, onions, and special sauce, then."

Wishbone's nose twitched. "I'd settle for just a plain one!"

Mr. Lee was smiling. "One burger, coming right up!" He slapped another patty on the grill. "How about a root beer to go with it?"

"Sure," Joe said. He looked at Wishbone. "Stay, boy. Stay." He let go of Wishbone's collar.

Wishbone gave Cap'n Ahab a warning look. The cat stared back from his one good eye. If cats did such a thing as sneer, the Cap'n was doing a good job of it. Wishbone sniffed. "Okay, pal, I'll let you off easy because you're a friend of Christy's. Only don't get pushy."

Cap'n Ahab yawned, showing at least fifty razor-sharp teeth.

Joe kept a close watch on Wishbone. He knew that the Jack Russell terrier wasn't afraid of anything— and that he did not like cats. To Joe's relief, though, Wishbone appeared to be doing his best to ignore Cap'n Ahab.

"Hey, Dad," Christy said as her father busied himself at the grill. "Joe found a copy of Hugo's poem about the pirate treasure."

Mr. Lee looked around from his cooking and smiled. "I'll bet you were excited."

Joe shrugged, feeling embarrassed. "I was at first. Then Christy told me that everyone already knew about it."

"I understand it caused a big stir nearly three-quarters of a century ago, when Hugo first found the poem," Mr. Lee said. "Too bad that the directions don't work. When people tried to use them to find Ben Walker's treasure, they got nowhere."

"Who was Ben Walker?" Joe asked.

"Oh, he was a famous buccaneer," Mr. Lee replied, turning the hamburger patty on the grill. "In the 1760s, St. George Bay was a sort of British outpost on the Gulf. It was once a Spanish town, but the Spanish pulled out around 1763. Anyway, lots of pirates used St. George Bay as a base. They raided ships in the Gulf, then sailed back here to spend their loot—or to hide it.

"Ben Walker was about the meanest of the pirates, as the legend goes. He had jet-black hair, a long black beard, and he was as bloodthirsty as they come. He sailed small, fast ships—sloops and schooners—but he never hesitated to attack larger vessels. Anyway, in 1765, the governor of Virginia sent pirate hunters after him. Walker wrecked one of his ships, the *Mad Mary's Revenge*, trying to get away from the government ships. They caught him, though, and put him in prison right here in town. He supposedly died of a fever before he ever came to trial."

Joe opened the old notebook. "I was sure that I'd found a clue to his treasure."

Mr. Lee was assembling the hamburger and its toppings. "Let's see." He glanced at the poem. "Yep! That's the famous Hugo Gilmore poem, all right. It names some real places. The Skeleton Reef Light, of course, and Faith Island, which is just offshore. The numbers and directions don't make any sense at all, though. Sorry. Still, you're not completely out of luck. You're getting a really great burger!" Mr. Lee handed his creation to Joe.

Joe took a bite of the hamburger, and then his eyes lit up. He swallowed. "This is delicious!"

"Thank you," said Mr. Lee with a broad smile. "The secret is the soy-based sauce! As we say around here . . ." He leaned toward his daughter, and together they said, "Oh, boy, it's the soy!"

"Whatever it is, it's great!" Joe happily munched his hamburger.

"Look at your dog," Christy said, laughing.

Joe glanced down. Wishbone was staring at him with a look of canine concentration. "What is it, Wishbone?"

Mr. Lee said solemnly, "I am an amateur dog psychologist. That dog is trying to send a telepathic message to you. Can't you feel it in your brain? He's trying to say, *'Feed the dog! Feed the dog! Feed the dog!'*"

Christy said, "Hey, Dad, how about a hot dog for Wishbone here?"

"Sweets to the sweet, eh?" Mr. Lee asked.

"I'll pay for it," Joe said.

"No, it's on the house," insisted Mr. Lee. "After all, I think Wishbone led you to us, and I know you're going to be a steady customer!" He reached into a bin with a pair of tongs and brought out a luscious-looking frankfurter. "Here you are, Wishbone." He slipped the frank onto a paper plate and handed it to Christy. She knelt and put the plate on the ground.

Wishbone was drooling in anticipation, but he looked up at Christy just a second too long.

"Cap'n Ahab! Bad cat!" Christy yelled.

Wishbone whipped his attention back to the paper plate. The cat had slipped up and had seized the frankfurter. Wishbone lunged forward—

"Wishbone, no!" Joe warned, hooking his finger through Wishbone's collar again.

Wishbone settled down with a disgusted grunt.

When Joe was sure that the dog wasn't going to charge, he let go of Wishbone's collar. "You weren't fast enough, boy."

Cap'n Ahab finished the frank in four quick bites. Then he leaped up, and Christy caught him. He purred and stared down at Wishbone with a narrow, yellow, one-eyed glare. His lip curled up on one side, revealing a long, sharp tooth.

Wishbone was quivering. Joe patted him. "Calm down, boy. You already had a hamburger."

Mr. Lee shook his head and handed Joe another frank. "Let Christy hang on to the Cap'n, and you give this to Wishbone," he suggested.

Joe leaned over and held out the hot dog. Wishbone sniffed it, took it, and gobbled it down. Joe ruffled his ears. "There you go. Share and share alike."

"Hey, Dad, look at the time," Christy said. "In fifteen minutes we need to be out at the place where they're building the new bank."

Mr. Lee switched off the grill, put his cooking utensils away, and took off his apron. "Right you are! Nice to have met you, Joe."

"Same here, sir. And the food really is great."

"Thank you!" Mr. Lee closed the window and went to the front of the RV. A second later he started the engine.

Christy said, "Would you like to go see where the pirate ship was wrecked back in 1765?"

"Sure," Joe said, feeling excited about the idea. Maybe, he thought, the poem *did* hold some kind of secret. Maybe no one had discovered it yet.

Somehow, the whole situation reminded him of one of the Sherlock Holmes stories he had read, "The Musgrave Ritual." Joe remembered how Sherlock Holmes had found a treasure no one else knew about in that story. And, Joe recalled, Holmes had told his friend Dr. Watson that the adventure was only the third case that he had ever tried to solve. Joe wondered if he could be as sharp as Holmes.

Anyway, Joe was more than willing to explore. He asked Christy, "How do we get there?"

"Easy. I've got my own boat! Today is Monday. I'm helping Dad tomorrow. But on Wednesday, I'll come by around ten in the morning. Okay?"

"Can Wishbone come?" Joe asked.

"Sure," Christy said. "Why not? I'll show you both all the sights around the bay."

She climbed into the RV's passenger's seat, and the vehicle clattered away down the drive.

Joe reached down to pet Wishbone. "Well," he said with a sigh, "it would be great if we could figure out the meaning of the poem. Maybe it has some kind of secret. If we could dig up a treasure, we could solve all of Wanda's restoration problems with the lighthouse." He scratched Wishbone's ears. "Oh, well, even if we don't discover any pirate loot, we did find a fine place to eat—and a friend."

Wishbone licked his chops. Then he growled softly.

Joe laughed. "Okay, a friend and a big orange cat. You don't have to be his buddy, but try to get along, okay?"

Wishbone sniffed, but he wagged his tail. Joe decided that his dog was trying to say he'd behave as long as the cat did.

Chapter Four

That night, Wishbone dreamed he was chasing Cap'n Ahab. But the cat he had tangled with during the day was now a cat-pirate, sailing a catamaran, a sailing ship with two hulls connected by struts. It was sort of like two canoes sitting side by side, connected with brackets. Wishbone was a brave pirate-hunter. He caught sight of the enemy craft in the first dog-watch and barked an order for his men to break out fresh sail. In the dream, Wishbone's ship came closer and closer to its prey. At the very last moment, peering ahead, Wishbone saw that the evil, one-eyed Cap'n Ahab had run the cannon out on board his pirate ship. Then, suddenly—

Boom! Boom! Boom!

Wishbone woke up with a yelp. "What happened? Am I shot?"

The booming sound came again. It was someone knocking on Joe's bedroom door. "Time to get up!" It was Rhonda's voice.

Joe sat up, mumbling, "Hmm? What? What's wrong?"

"Time to get up! You have five minutes! Shorts, T-shirt, and sneakers! Get moving, Mr. Talbot!"

With woozy eyes, Joe blinked at the clock. "It's only six in the morning!"

Wishbone was still recovering from the shock of his dream. "Maybe the house is on fire! Maybe pirate cats have raided the coast! No, that's silly. I know—maybe breakfast is ready!" He perked up immediately.

Feeling only half-awake, Joe got out of bed and dressed. He and Wishbone went downstairs. Ellen, wearing jogging shorts, a T-shirt, and a headband, gave her son an "I'm sorry" sort of look.

"What's up, Mom?" Joe asked, trying to keep from yawning.

Ellen sighed. "Aerobics," she said. "Wanda's cousin Rhonda is convinced that we all need lots of exercise."

"This early?" Joe asked in surprise.

Rhonda came downstairs, leading a protesting

42

Wanda. Wanda was decked out in some sweats that were too big for her. "Really," she was saying, "I can't wear your clothes. That's just not polite."

"Come along," Rhonda commanded. "Carperdale is waiting."

Joe followed them into the yard. He had to admit it was a beautiful day. Early morning dew sparkled on the grass, and birds were twittering in the live oaks and in the tops of the palms. Joe took a deep breath. The air smelled salty and clean, and a refreshing breeze was blowing.

Carperdale, dressed in a sweatshirt and tan slacks, was waiting with a boom box. "Ready, madam?" he asked politely.

Rhonda held up a hand. "In just a minute. First we stretch. Everyone, follow me." She led them all through a series of muscle-stretching routines. Carperdale followed along gamely. Joe thought he had just discovered why Carperdale was so trim and active, even though he was elderly. An exercise routine like that every morning would keep anyone in good condition.

Even Wishbone got into the act, pushing his front paws way out front, stretching his spine.

Rhonda pointed at Wishbone and laughed. "I like to see a dog who keeps in shape!"

"This was wonderful, Rhonda," Wanda said, puffing, as they wound up the stretches. "Let's do it again tomorrow—only later in the day."

Rhonda wagged a finger at her cousin. "We're not finished yet, Wanda. In fact, we've just started. Let her rip, Carperdale!" The elderly gentleman switched on the boom box. Music pounded out of it, music with a steady, fast beat. Rhonda lined Joe, Ellen, and Wanda up and then faced them. "All right. Let's begin with

43

jumping jacks! We'll take it easy—only a hundred to start with!"

She began to lead them, jumping, scissoring her legs, and clapping her hands over her head. Carperdale joined right in. Joe could not help grinning. He had never seen anyone do jumping jacks with such dignity!

Beside Joe, Wanda groaned, but she followed along. "Come on," Ellen urged with a laugh. "Look—even Wishbone has worked out a set of exercises!"

On the other side of Joe, Wishbone was leaping, turning, twisting, crouching, twirling, and leaping again.

"At least someone's having fun," Wanda said in an out-of-breath voice.

Joe was feeling better and more wide awake. He enjoyed the cool air, the springy feel of the sandy soil, and the fresh sea breeze.

Rhonda pointed at him. "Joe's got the beat! Nothing like this to get the old heart rate up! Come on, Wanda, you slowpoke! Even the little dog is keeping up!"

Ellen panted, saying, "Don't call him 'little'! I think Wishbone believes he's exactly the right size!"

Soon only Joe, who was a well-toned boy and who was in great shape from playing basketball, was able to keep up with Rhonda and Carperdale without missing a beat. When ten minutes had passed, Wishbone seemed to think his own workout was complete. He stretched out on the lawn, panting.

After half an hour, Rhonda nodded to Carperdale, and he switched off the music. "Rather vigorous today, madam," he observed, patting his brow with an immaculate white handkerchief.

"Well, it was pretty fair," Rhonda said. "Tomorrow we'll start to push it a little harder."

"Tomorrow?" Wanda groaned.

"Now you've got half an hour to shower, and then breakfast will be served. March!"

Joe took a shower and then put on fresh clothes. Wishbone had plopped down next to the bed, looking as if he enjoyed the cool parquet floor against his tummy. The old notebook that Joe had found in the tower was on the foot of the bed. As he sat down to put on his sneakers, Joe reached for the book, and Wishbone looked up at him.

"I keep thinking about 'The Musgrave Ritual,'" Joe told Wishbone. He picked up the Sherlock Holmes paperback from the bedside table and glanced at the story again, remembering its plot.

Reginald Musgrave, a college friend of Sherlock Holmes, asked the detective to look into the mysterious disappearance of a butler. Holmes learned that the family had an old ceremony that the butler had been interested in. The ritual had all sorts of silly-sounding questions and answers in it: "Whose was it?" "His who is gone." "Who shall have it?" "He who will come." There were other puzzling phrases like that. Sherlock Holmes had to try really hard before he finally figured out that the questions were clues.

Joe said thoughtfully, "Maybe no one has thought of the right questions about the Skeleton Reef poem yet. Well, boy, you and I will just have to try our best!"

As soon as Joe was ready, he and Wishbone went downstairs to breakfast. Rhonda served Joe a tall, chilled glass of freshly squeezed orange juice, some cold cereal with delicious wild blueberries, two pieces of homemade whole-wheat bread, and a pot of grape jam. Joe ate with enthusiasm. The exercise, he decided, had given him quite an appetite.

Wishbone, too, seemed even hungrier than usual. He got to eat right in the dining room, near the table. Rhonda had thoughtfully provided him with one deep bowl full of crunchy dry dog food, and another with cool water. Wishbone dug in, looking very pleased indeed.

"I'm going to ache all over," Wanda complained. "I ought to be trying to find some way out of this horrible mess, not jumping around on your front lawn at six o'clock in the morning."

Rhonda patted her hand. "Dear, you won't be able to do anything if you let yourself get run-down. Besides, look at your friends. How do you feel, Ellen?"

Ellen suddenly sat straighter in her chair and opened her eyes wide. "Oh, great!" she said quickly, though Joe thought she still looked out of breath.

Rhonda beamed. "Joe, how about you?"

"Fine," Joe said. "It was a good workout."

"There you are," Rhonda said. "Now, when you finish, we'll run into town—"

"Run?" Wanda asked, turning pale.

Rolling her eyes, Rhonda said, "Just a figure of speech. All right, we'll *drive* into town in the Rolls. I have a boat at the marina, and we'll take a spin out to the lighthouse. You may as well see what you're up against, Wanda."

"*Drive* into town. I like the sound of that," Wanda replied with relief.

Joe was psyched at the thought of riding in such a cool car. The inside of the Rolls-Royce was just as impressive as the outside. It was roomy enough for all of them, and it smelled of the finest, softest leather and polish. The big engine purred as the car moved along quietly. Wishbone, sitting on Joe's lap, looked out the window. Joe, too, studied the town again as they drove through. It was a strange mixture of modern and old buildings, crooked streets, and shaggy-topped palm trees.

Carperdale dropped off the group at a marina. Rhonda led the way down to the end of a pier.

Wanda gasped. "Not a rowboat!" She was staring at a dory, similar to a rowboat. It was a weathered-gray color. On the stern was the name *Rhonda's Pet.*

"No," Rhonda said regretfully. "It's too small. We're going in this." She led them aboard a twenty-foot motorboat, this one named *Fit as a Fiddle.* She handed out orange life jackets and even found a small one that fit Wishbone.

Ellen ruffled Wishbone's ears. "You know, orange isn't really his color, but a handsome dog looks good in anything." Wishbone seemed to grin at the compliment.

With a tug on the pull-cord, Rhonda started the outboard motor. Sitting in the stern, she steered them away from the dock. "We're early," she shouted over the motor's noise. "Just a few fishermen are out right now. Soon the bay will be full of boats."

Wishbone's tail was wagging furiously. Joe chuckled as he held on to his buddy. He leaned back and enjoyed the cool breeze and the salty sea spray. This was a great vacation!

Rhonda pointed across the bay. "The river empties in the Gulf over there. See the two little islands? They're Faith and Hope."

Joe craned his neck to look where she was pointing. The islands were very low green mounds, hardly showing above the waterline. Ahead of them loomed the lighthouse.

"You can see more of the reef today," Ellen said.

Joe saw the oyster sandbar. Its dark gray surface was covered with oyster shells, and it looked as rough as the bark of an ancient tree.

Rhonda nodded. "The tide's lower. Okay, while we're on the way, I'll give you a little history lesson. There's been a lighthouse on Skeleton Reef ever since 1688, when the Spanish built a wooden tower there. That one blew away in a storm, but the British built a brick tower there in 1763. According to legend, its light went out only twice. The first time was on the wild, stormy night in 1765, when Ben Walker's pirate ship was wrecked on the reef."

"That's why the poem says 'Devil take the keeper o' the Skeleton Reef Light,'" Joe said. He had told them all about the poem. Rhonda had agreed with Christy and her dad. She felt that the poem was interesting, but that it really didn't lead to treasure.

"That's right," Rhonda told Joe. "Old Walker blamed the lighthouse keeper for the loss of his sloop, the *Mad Mary's Revenge*. The stories say that the old pirate had thousands of dollars' worth of gold and jewels in her cargo hold. But she sank in the bay, and no one ever found the exact spot."

"We could sure use that money now," Wanda said. "Two hundred and fifty thousand dollars, to be exact!"

Rhonda guided the boat in a sweeping curve that led them farther and farther away from shore. Early morning fishing crews seemed to recognize her. They waved or called out to her in a friendly way. She slowed the boat as they came closer to the lighthouse. "We have to be careful now. There's a channel that will let us tie up at the base of the lighthouse, but the water is very shallow all around. Even this little boat could grind up onto the reef."

Wanda was shaking her head, with one hand clapped to her hat to hold it on in the breeze. "The lighthouse doesn't look in very good shape from here."

It was true. The gray bricks looked crumbly. From where they were, Joe saw that the windowpanes were cracked and broken. Reddish-orange streaks of rust ran down from the cone-shaped metal roof and the fittings around the glassed-in lamp chamber just beneath. In the early morning sunlight, the lighthouse looked sad and lonely.

"It's almost two hundred and forty years old," Wanda said sadly. "Oh, I hope we can come up with a way to save it."

Rhonda slowed the boat still more. They were barely puttering along. "Well, cousin, *parts* of it are nearly two hundred and forty years old—the lower portions. The top was replaced. That happened the second time the light went out—and that lasted for five whole years. You see, in the Civil War, the Confederate Navy tried to blow up the lighthouse because it served as a landmark for Union ships. The plan didn't quite succeed. Oh, the dynamite blasted off the top of the tower, so the light was useless, but the base remained. Then after the Civil War, the Windom family rebuilt the lighthouse. They made it even better than before. Still, I think the newest part of the lighthouse—that would be the electric light—is at least seventy-five years old."

"It's history decaying away," Wanda moaned.

Sounding as if she were trying to cheer up her cousin, Rhonda said, "Well, it isn't gone yet. Of course, I never saw the lighthouse in operation, but I understand it had a twenty-thousand-candlepower lamp— that's a light as bright as twenty thousand candles burning all at once, Joe. Sailors could see the beam from as far out as sixteen miles at sea. It must have been quite a sight."

By now, they were only a few dozen yards away from their destination. Interested and curious, Joe asked, "Can we actually go inside the lighthouse?"

Rhonda shook her head. "Better not. It's not really safe. There hasn't even been a keeper here for . . . oh . . . nearly fifty years. Still, we can walk around the base and have a good look. Maybe we can even open the door and just take a peek inside. I don't think that would be a problem."

Slowly, Rhonda eased the motorboat through the channel. She explained that the lighthouse had once rested on a large concrete base. Next to it had been a little cottage, the lighthouse keepers' home. "That blew away in a big hurricane years ago," she said with a sigh. "A good part of the outer concrete base was broken up and washed away at the same time. Now, just the section that sits directly under the lighthouse is left.

"After the hurricane, the men who worked as the keepers over the years started staying in the base of the tower itself when they had to. Most days, though, a keeper would just row out, the way we're doing now, and he kept the light going all night. Then he would return to shore. When it was stormy, however, he stayed out here and used a cot and a little stove inside the tower. He remained with the light as long as he needed to."

"Are any of the keepers still around?" Joe asked.

Rhonda shook her head. "I don't think so. There were dozens of them over the years, of course. A lot of them came from one local family, too; they were cousins of the Windom family. I suppose the last real lighthouse keeper died twenty years ago or more. Joe, get ready to jump out. Can you tie a good knot?"

"Sure."

"Then get the bowline—that rope there—and tie us up to one of the cleats when I tell you. Ready? Jump!"

Joe leaped onto the concrete platform, and Wishbone followed. Joe felt dizzy after the movement of the boat. He and Wishbone were only about two feet above the water, and the incoming waves gurgled and swirled just under them. Straining to reach, Joe took the rope and was about to tie it to the metal cleat, bolted to the concrete, when something boomed behind him, making his heart leap into his throat.

He and Wishbone whirled around. The metal door at the base of the lighthouse had banged open. Standing there with one hand on the door was a gray-haired, glaring man. He was short and muscular, wearing jeans and a dark blue jacket. "Get off my light!" he roared.

Wishbone yipped. Joe felt his heart thud. His first thought, quite a wild idea, was that a ghost had appeared. He stammered, "I-I . . . w-was ju-just tying—"

"Get back in the boat, Joe! Never mind the bowline!" Rhonda's voice was sharp and urgent. Joe jumped back down into the boat, and he picked up Wishbone and helped him down, too.

The old man stalked forward. "Don't come back!" he thundered.

"Mr. Bevans, that's not very neighborly," Rhonda snapped. "We're leaving, but you don't own the lighthouse—"

The man leaned over and shoved at the bow of the boat, pushing it away. Then he stood up straight and shook his fist. "Never come back! Doom waits for ye if ye set foot on Skeleton Reef! Doom, do ye hear? Doom, I say!"

Wanda wore a strained smile, her teeth clenched. Through them she muttered, "Oh, Rhonda, I'd say it would be a good plan to leave now."

Rhonda maneuvered the boat around and they started to putter away. Joe looked over his shoulder. "Don't pay any attention to him," Rhonda said in a quiet voice. "He's a town character, one of the cousins of the Windoms I was talking about. He's not all there, if you understand me."

The man was still on the platform, continuing to shake his fist. Across the water, his hoarse voice again carried its dire warning: "Doom! Doom for ye all! Doom, I say! *Do-o-oom!*"

Chapter Five

"Who *was* that?" Joe asked for the third time. The group had retreated to the town of St. George Bay. Rhonda had avoided talking about the scary man at the lighthouse. She had taken her guests on a tour of Market Street, which had lots of art galleries and quaint antiques shops. They had strolled through the Municipal Garden behind the United Methodist Church. Rhonda had pointed out special roses as well as oleanders, mimosa, and other exotic flowers. Wishbone had examined quite a few unknown varieties of bushes.

Very little of the town tour mattered to Joe. He was burning to know more about the strange man at the tower. Finally the group had walked up Water Street to the Cool Shoppe, where Rhonda had treated them all to ice-cream sundaes at a sidewalk table. That was when Joe asked about the man again.

Rhonda sighed. "Oh, well, after that little scene, I suppose you all do have a right to know about him. He's a local character, as I said. His name is Nathaniel Bevans. He lives over at the end of Bay Street in a run-down little house with a canal just behind it that leads into the bay. I don't think Mr. Bevans is really dangerous—at least, I've never heard of him ever hurting anyone—but he's a little off."

Ellen stopped eating her sundae, her spoon an inch above the ice-cream treat. She looked a bit alarmed. "What do you mean, he's 'off'? In what way?"

With a shrug, Rhonda replied, "He says his family has always supplied the keepers for the Skeleton Reef Light. According to him, the very first lighthouse keeper was his great-umpty-great-grandfather or something. All the others have been cousins, or so he says. It may be true—the Bevans family are cousins of the Windoms. All I know for sure is that Mr. Bevans thinks he's the last of the lighthouse keepers."

Joe shook his head. He didn't think a keeper should scare the wits out of visitors!

Wanda swallowed a gloopy spoonful of ice cream and fudge sauce. "I don't understand. How could the lighthouse even need a keeper? I thought you said that the Skeleton Reef Light has been closed for around fifty years."

"Yes, it has," Rhonda said. "And that's about how old Mr. Bevans is, too, so he can't be the official keeper. I've heard stories around town, though. According to gossip, Mr. Bevans's father *did* work as the lighthouse keeper a long time ago, back before World War II. I suppose that's why Mr. Bevans has got it in his head that the Skeleton Reef Light is his responsibility. In real life, though, he's always earned his living as a fishing guide or a merchant seaman. The government closed the lighthouse just about the time when he was born."

Wishbone, lying on his tummy in the warm sunlight, stretched and yawned. Joe reached down to scratch his ears. As he straightened again, Joe asked,

"How did he get out to the lighthouse? I didn't see any other boats out there."

"Oh, it was there," Rhonda assured him. "Mr. Bevans has a flat-bottomed boat, a scow, with a little electric trolling motor on it. It draws only a few inches of water." She must have noticed Joe's puzzled expression, so she explained, "That means his boat floats high, with only about five or six inches of its bottom under the water's surface. He can float right over the oyster reef. His electric motor runs very quietly, so he can sneak right up on you if you're not watching. I'm sure his scow was tied up on the other side of the lighthouse."

Wanda dabbed at her lips with a napkin. "It's a shame he's just a fishing guide. If he were a rich eccentric, he might be of some help with the restoration. He seems to like the lighthouse enough!"

"I don't know if that's the right way of putting it," Rhonda said. "Maybe he's *obsessed* with it. As you heard, he thinks the lighthouse brings bad luck. He doesn't hesitate to tell anyone that doom will come to them even just by visiting the lighthouse—unless, of course, your name happens to be Nathaniel Bevans. He shows up out there now and again. Sometimes you can see him up in the light chamber, looking around the bay through a brass telescope."

Joe felt a surge of curiosity. "Why would he do that? What's he looking for?"

Rhonda shook her head. "With an eccentric like that, who knows? Well, he won't be there all the time! We'll go back some other day."

They left the sidewalk table and headed back to the marina parking lot, where Carperdale was supposed to pick them up at ten. They were a little early. While Ellen, Wanda, and Rhonda stood and chatted, Joe and Wishbone walked down to the docks.

Sailboats, cabin cruisers, and fishing boats were floating on the blue-green water of the Gulf. Black-capped laughing gulls soared and wheeled in the sky and gave their strange calls. They sounded like small children having a terrific case of the giggles. Joe watched some people climb aboard a sailboat called the *Wave Dancer*.

As they got the boat under way, Joe looked past them, at the Skeleton Reef Light. In the glassed-in light chamber he could see a dark figure. Joe guessed it was Mr. Bevans. Just as Rhonda had described, Bevans seemed to be gazing out at the shore with a telescope. Joe wondered if the man had been staring at him and Wishbone, and he got that creepy feeling of goose bumps running down his spine. In a quiet voice, he said, "Come on, Wishbone."

Wishbone had been sniffing his way around the foot of the docks. Small white crabs lived in burrows that they dug into the sand near the water. They scuttled over the sand as silent as shadows and as fast as lightning. Wishbone barked at one and it sped away.

56

Joe took a step toward him. "That's a ghost crab, Wishbone. You can't catch them. Even if you did corner one, he'd nip your nose hard!" He looked back at the lighthouse. He could not tell for sure, but it seemed as if Mr. Bevans might have turned his spyglass right on Joe and Wishbone. With more urgency in his voice, Joe called, "Here, boy! Come on, Wishbone!"

Obediently, the Jack Russell terrier trotted over and sat looking up expectantly at Joe.

Joe was staring at the lighthouse. The dark figure moved to one side. Joe could see that he was looking elsewhere with his telescope. Breathing a sigh of relief, Joe could not help but think how the Skeleton Reef Light resembled the tower of an ancient castle.

That made Joe remember again the Sherlock Holmes story "The Musgrave Ritual." He pulled a piece of folded paper from his shirt pocket, opened it, and read it. It was a copy of the poem that Hugo J. Gilmore, Jr., had written down in 1922. He looked at the stanza that first mentioned numbers:

Bear down ten, bear another five,
Hope for luck, and three and thirty;
Then larboard, seven and twenty strive.
'Tis gold, 'tis gold, ye seek for charity,
Three Sisters will guard it there for ye.
Seek when the moon be shining bright,
And Devil take the keeper o' the Skeleton
  Reef Light!

There was more, but none of it made sense. Joe read the words of that stanza slowly, aloud. Then he looked at Wishbone. He could not help laughing at his dog's inquisitive expression. "Can't figure it out, either, can you, boy?"

Wishbone gave himself a good shake.

Joe shook his head. "I don't know. It doesn't *read* like nonsense. Those numbers are too precise for the poem to be just a joke. It has to be a mystery, like the one about the missing butler that Sherlock Holmes solved."

"Joe!" Ellen was calling.

Joe turned and saw that Carperdale had pulled the big burgundy Rolls-Royce into the parking lot. "Race you to the car, Wishbone!"

Wishbone was always ready for a race. He easily passed Joe. When he reached the parked car, Wishbone spun and grinned. Joe pulled up, laughing, and said, "I guess four legs can always beat two, huh, boy?"

Wishbone smiled, his tongue hanging out.

As Joe was getting into the car, he paused. "Uh . . . Mr. Carperdale? . . ."

Carperdale was holding the door open. "Yes, Joseph?"

"What do you think about the poem that Hugo Gilmore found back in 1922? Was it a fake?"

Carperdale raised one eyebrow, his eyes twinkling. "I worked for Mr. Hugo for thirty years, Joseph. He was my friend, as well as my employer. In all that time, I often heard him speak of finding that puzzling rhyme. All I can tell you is that he believed in it."

"What about you?"

"I believed in Mr. Hugo. . . . Climb in, if you please, sir, and we'll have a nice drive back home."

A few minutes after noon, Wishbone was excited when Mr. Lee's lunch wagon showed up again at Rhonda's house. This time, however, Christy hadn't come along. "She's helping at the main restaurant," Mr. Lee explained to Joe and Wishbone. "One of the waitresses has the day off today."

Wishbone took a deep, suspicious sniff. "Too bad about missing Christy, Joe. At least there's some good news. That pirate cat isn't here today, either, the little sausage snatcher!"

Joe helped Mr. Lee by taking lunch orders from the painters, who were almost finished on the second floor. Since Rhonda was taking all of her guests into town for lunch, Joe turned down Mr. Lee's offer of another burger. Wishbone sighed regretfully. He, too, appreciated the tasty secret-soy-sauce burgers. And today there was no thieving cat to steal a burger or a juicy frankfurter from a handsome and hungry dog!

After Joe delivered the hamburgers to the painters, he found Carperdale. The caretaker had changed from paint-spattered overalls to his customary crisp khaki uniform.

Carperdale seemed to sense that Joe had something on his mind. "Yes, Joseph?" he asked politely as the two of them walked downstairs.

"I was wondering what you could tell me about Mr. Bevans," Joe said. They paused in the hallway. Carperdale didn't say anything for a moment, and Joe added, "I think he's strange, the way he stands up in the lighthouse with his telescope and spies on people. He seems a little . . . well, a little scary."

Wishbone cocked his head. "I can tell you he startled the daylights out of me! He popped out of that lighthouse like the ghost appearing on the castle battlements in *Hamlet!*"

Carperdale looked very serious. He stroked his moustache, as if making sure the ends were curled just right. "Hmm . . . I'm sure you have good reasons for asking, but I really don't know much about the fellow. I will tell you this, Joseph—do not go near Mr. Nathaniel Bevans. He is quarrelsome, unpleasant, and bad-tempered. Aside from that, I need say no more. A gentleman never spreads idle gossip."

Wishbone sighed. "We never get to hear the juicy stuff!"

Carperdale drove everyone back into town. Wishbone enjoyed the luxurious interior of the car, filling his nose with the rich scents of leather and walnut. "Ah, the world's finest limousine—and an expert chauffeur! This is the life! Just call me a happy, pampered pooch!"

Rhonda had made an appointment for Wanda to speak to Mr. West and to Mrs. Xavier of the St. George Lighthouse Preservation Society. It was a luncheon appointment at the Sea Oats Inn, a hotel and restaurant near the waterfront.

According to its sign, the Sea Oats had been built way back in 1945. The inn was a big, three-story frame house, surrounded by a wraparound veranda. Sprinklers shot jets of water over the hotel's lush green lawn. On either side of the walkway to the front steps, a double row of date palms played host to buzzing, plump, slow-moving bumblebees. Wishbone had to admire the handsome old building. Dark blue shutters guarded every window. The rest of the inn was painted sea-blue and cream-white. The dining room, which was inside on the first floor facing the veranda, did not allow dogs.

Rhonda spoke to one of the owners, and the lady allowed Joe to tie Wishbone's leash to an old anchor that served as a decoration on the wide veranda of the hotel. It was a cool, comfortable, shady spot, with a nice breeze sweeping in off the Gulf.

The refreshing sea air carried the scents of salt water, fish, and scuttling little ghost crabs. The outdoor smells almost hid the mouth-watering aromas of lobster, shrimp, and oysters that leaked from the dining room. As Joe tied Wishbone up, he said, "Be good, boy. I'll keep an eye on you from just inside."

Wishbone looked up hopefully. "If I'm *very* good, could you possibly smuggle out a steak or two? Wait, how about just a nice soup bone? Or even a deviled crab would do! . . . Joe?" No use—Joe had already gone inside. "Oh, well, I'll just lie down here and make sure no cats come around. Nothing can spoil a good lunch like a cat hanging around waiting for a handout. Cats are so *greedy.*"

Wishbone gave up hoping for a snack. He stretched out next to the set of French doors that led from the porch into the dining room. Resting his chin on his front paws and closing his eyes, he appeared to doze. In reality, thanks to his exceptionally fine hearing, Wishbone was listening hard to every word that was spoken at his friends' table.

Mr. West, a heavyset, bald man with a very red face, told Wanda he was sorry, but the society simply lacked the money to renovate the lighthouse. Mrs. Xavier, thin and white-haired and nervous-sounding, agreed. It was too bad that St. George Bay didn't have a bigger population to help pay the cost. Perhaps the lighthouse could be made into a tourist site. Unfortunately, there wasn't time.

From the conversation, it was clear to Wishbone that neither a population explosion nor the creation of a Lighthouse Land attraction was practical. He heard Mr. West say that the lighthouse had been condemned for nearly two years already; time was quickly running out to save it. The preservation society had tried everything, but so far nothing had worked. It seemed that the lighthouse was doomed.

Wishbone closed his eyes. The situation was desperate. He wondered what would happen if the city of St. George Bay forced the Oakdale Historical Society to pay for tearing down the lighthouse. Would Wanda be ruined? Would she have to sell her house and move away?

That could never happen. Wishbone couldn't let it happen! *After all*, he thought sternly, *if Wanda has to move, the next person to live in her house may not plant flowers. And without her flowerbeds, where would I bury all my stuff? Anyway, I've put a lot of time into training Wanda. I'd hate to have to start from scratch with a new person.*

There had to be a way to help Joe help Wanda, Wishbone decided. And he knew that the burden of finding that way would be on his own doggy shoulders!

Wishbone had made up his mind. He would put his intelligence on the problem right away. As Sherlock Holmes would say, "There is not a moment to lose. The game is afoot!"

Chapter Six

That evening after dinner, Joe sat quietly, watching Wanda work at Rhonda's dining room table. She had scattered papers, pencils, and a calculator all around her. As Ellen, Rhonda, Joe, and Wishbone looked on, Wanda punched the calculator keys, sighed, scribbled numbers on a page, then tried again.

Joe had never seen Wanda look so miserable—not even when she was scolding Wishbone for digging up her nasturtiums. She clenched a yellow pencil in her teeth and sniffled now and then. She shook her head every time she looked at the columns of revised figures. Finally, she took the pencil from her mouth, made a last note, and looked up. She was smiling, but Joe thought her expression was anything but happy.

"Well," she said, her voice pretend-cheerful, "I think I have it all figured out. The Oakdale Historical Society can put every cent of its money in the pot. The St. George Lighthouse Preservation Society can chip in all it has. I'll contribute all my savings, and I'll sell my car. Cousin Rhonda, you told me you could contribute about five thousand dollars. Well, if we can really do all that . . ."—she began to sniffle—". . . if we can *really* do it, we can just about afford to have the lighthouse torn down!"

Ellen patted her friend's hand. "Oh, Wanda, no!"

"We can't let you do that," Rhonda said loyally.

A tear rolled down Wanda's cheek. "Thank you, but I really don't see any other way out. Oh, what am I going to do? I've ruined the Oakdale Historical Society, and I've messed up all my friends' lives!"

Joe cleared his throat. "Uh . . . you know, there *is* the treasure."

Rhonda shook her head, smiling sadly. "Joe, I've told you there is no treasure. Great-Uncle Hugo would have found it if it ever really existed. Or the hundreds of other treasure hunters would have found it. That poem must have been a hoax."

"Who would have gone to all that trouble?" Joe asked.

Rhonda shrugged. "Well, in 1922, Hugo was all of ten years old. I have known ten-year-old boys who were very mischievous. Hugo was also very bright. He could have made up that poem all by himself."

Joe thought about that. "The poem was supposed to be carved on the underside of an old wooden bed frame. When would Hugo have been able to do that? When could a ten-year-old have snuck into the jail to carve it?"

Ellen raised her eyebrows. "You have a point, Joe."

Wishbone sat up, ears alert, as if he were following every word.

With a shrug, Rhonda said, "I suppose Hugo couldn't have carved the poem into the wood. I'm afraid, though, that no one remembers seeing that bed frame. It might simply all have been a tale that Hugo invented."

Joe pressed his lips together. He remembered what

64

Carperdale had said: "I believed in Mr. Hugo." Some-how, Joe believed in old Hugo, too. In Joe's bones, he knew that he couldn't just forget about the poem.

Later that evening in his room, Joe opened his window and stood for a while in the dark, looking out over the bay. A bright moon made the Gulf water sparkle with silver flashes. The breeze brought in the salty smell of the Gulf, and Joe took a deep, thoughtful breath. Red and green lights twinkled aboard boats out at sea. On the far horizon, lightning flickered inside towering thunderheads. The summer storms out in the Gulf were so distant that Joe could not hear even the slightest grumble of thunder.

He closed the window and turned on the lamp beside his bed. He sat on the edge of the bed and read the poem again. Wishbone jumped up on the bed and rested his chin on Joe's leg, making a warm spot there. Joe patted his head. "I know the answer's here," he said. "It has to be. So what if Hugo was just a kid when he wrote this?"

Wishbone licked Joe's hand reassuringly.

"I don't think he'd invent all these details. The poem doesn't *sound* as if a kid wrote it. I wonder what happened to the wood that had the original poem carved on it."

Wishbone sighed.

"Carperdale might know," Joe said. "I'll ask him, anyway. If he can't help us, maybe Christy could find out from some of the people in town. What do you say, Wishbone? If a kid started this mystery, do you think a couple of kids can solve it?"

Wishbone licked his hand. Joe took that as a "yes."

"We'll start tomorrow," Joe said, turning off the light and getting under the sheet. "Bright and early. Right after our exercise routine with Rhonda, maybe."

Wishbone walked in a circle three times and then settled down for the night.

They fell asleep to the distant sound of low waves breaking on the beach. It was a peaceful, soothing sound, and it gave Joe a night of deep and restful sleep.

The next morning brought another round of vigorous aerobics, led by Rhonda. Afterward, with Wishbone panting beside him, Joe offered to carry the boom box inside for Carperdale. He had something he wanted to ask the chauffeur. "Did you ever see the wood that had the poem carved on it?" Joe asked.

Carperdale gave Joe a strange look. "I am not *that* old, Joseph. I began to work for Mr. Hugo when he was already a middle-aged man. The discovery was many years before my time. Just put the sound device here, please." He opened a hall closet and indicated a shelf.

Joe slipped the boom box onto the shelf. "I know. Hugo was only about ten years old when he found the poem, but I thought he might have told you about it."

"Ah," Carperdale said, brushing his moustache. "Quite right. He often told me about how excited everyone in town was when the discovery first became known. Practically the whole population became treasure hunters. People were running about with spades and pickaxes. Each one of them had a favorite location for digging. Mr. Hugo told me that his father became quite upset. In his opinion, the poem led only to a lot of irritation, useless activity, and unsightly holes dug all around. Mr. Hugo's father had no patience at all with visitors who excavated his flower gardens."

Wishbone scratched an ear. Joe grinned and said, "Wanda's the same way when Wishbone starts digging in her yard. It must be a family trait. Did Hugo ever say anything about the carving?"

Carperdale sighed. "Only that his father had hidden it away somewhere, just to prevent more people making a nuisance of themselves. However, Mr. Hugo insisted he had made an accurate copy. You had better go up and get ready for breakfast now. I shall be serving some very tasty waffles with whipped cream and fresh strawberries in precisely five and a half minutes."

Breakfast was tasty. Afterward, while Joe waited for Christy to come by, he decided he would explore the old house a little more. Like most houses close to the water, it had no basement, so Joe and Wishbone began to look around on the first floor. They checked out the parlor and the dining room, the kitchen and the pantry (which seemed to interest Wishbone a lot). They inspected the library, a study with a massive round oak table in the center and two walls with floor-to-ceiling bookcases built in. Wishbone sniffed at the spines of some of the old leather-bound books and sneezed.

Joe chuckled. He twitched his nose, because the strange, spicy dust of old books was tickling his nostrils, too. He looked at the titles. Seven whole shelves were filled with tightly packed tan volumes that were all identical. Their spines read, *Annual Statistics of Commercial Fishing*. Each one covered a single year. The earliest, way up on a top shelf, was from 1802; the latest one, seven shelves down and over on the right, was dated 1966.

Joe wondered briefly who would be interested in more than a hundred and fifty fat volumes of fishing statistics. Maybe a real fishing nut, he decided. Wishbone sniffed the spines of the lower books, but the look he gave Joe was as blank as the way Joe felt.

Next to the library were Carperdale's rooms. Joe did not look inside them. Next, there was a bathroom, the front hall, and the hall closet. Then came a formal living room with tall windows that looked out over the back lawn, down a long slope, to the Gulf. The water was sparkling and blue that morning. Lots of fluffy white clouds scooted across the sky from right to left. Joe could see whitecaps out on the water.

He heard someone come downstairs and went to the hall to see who it was. He found Wanda, Rhonda, and Ellen. "I've got to try," Wanda was saying. She had a look of determination in her eyes.

"Hi," Joe said. "What's up?"

"Cousin Wanda is going into town to talk to the city council," Rhonda said. "I've already told her it won't do any good."

"It might," Wanda insisted.

"All right," Rhonda said. "Still, you could at least let Carperdale drive you there."

"No. He's busy with the painters," Wanda said. "That's why I called a cab." The car came rattling into the drive just then; it was a battered yellow taxi. Wanda sighed. "Wish me luck," she said. Then she went outside and climbed into the cab. A moment later the taxi turned and clattered away.

"Poor Wanda," Ellen said. "You don't think she has much of a chance, do you?"

Rhonda shook her head. "The commissioners are pretty stubborn. The only way they'd change their minds would be if some earthshaking event occurred. Of course, Wanda might manage to get an extension of the deadline. She can be pretty persuasive."

Joe saw a solitary figure cycling into the drive. "Mom," he said, "here comes Christy Lee. She sort of promised to show me around town and maybe even take me out on her boat. Do you mind if Wishbone and I go with her?"

"I don't know. I haven't met Christy," Ellen said. "Where will you be going?"

Rhonda said, "Oh, heavens, Ellen, don't worry. Christy is a good, no-nonsense girl. She has loads of common sense, and she's an excellent sailor. Besides, St. George Bay is a very law-abiding town. They'll be perfectly safe."

"All right," Ellen said, smiling. "I don't suppose you can get into too much trouble around here."

"You'll need transportation, though," Rhonda added. "I rented the tandem bikes for the whole week. Why don't you and Christy take one of them?"

By then Christy had parked her bike and climbed off it. She was wearing a red baseball cap, red cut-off shorts, and a baggy yellow T-shirt. She had a heavy-looking backpack on. Joe met her at the front steps. She agreed right away to try out the tandem bike.

"Cool," Christy said. "I've never been on one. Can I steer?"

"Let's take the blue one," Joe said. "Wishbone seems to enjoy riding in the basket."

He helped Wishbone get in. Then he climbed onto the seat behind Christy's. They got off to a wobbly start out of the drive. Soon, though, Christy got the hang of it. They zoomed along the bike path toward town.

From his position in the basket, Wishbone enjoyed every second of the ride. *This is the way to travel*, he thought. *Out in the open, with the wind fluffing your fur! The warm breeze in your face! The smells of nature all*

around! Not to mention the mouth-watering aromas of seafood restaurants, hot-dog stands, and cotton candy!

Wishbone heard Joe ask, "Uh . . . Christy? Do you think we could find some way to sort of explore the old lighthouse?"

Christy laughed. "That poem has really had an effect on you, hasn't it?"

"Well, yes," Joe admitted.

"It's just summer-folk foolishness," Christy said. "If there was anything to it, the treasure would have been found years ago."

"That's what Rhonda says, too," Joe admitted.

"Well, it's something to do," Christy said. "Have you ever been on a sailboat before?"

Wishbone perked up his ears. "Sailboat? We can go on a sailboat?"

Joe said, "No, I guess I haven't."

"Okay," Christy said. "I've got a little catamaran

70

called the *Suncatcher*. I'll give you some pointers first. Then we'll sail out to the lighthouse. Don't expect too much. It's in terrible shape."

"I know. Still, the poem says—"

"Oh, come on, Joe," Christy teased. "Forget that poem! It's nothing but very bad rhyming—doggerel, my dad calls it."

Wishbone sniffed to himself. Doggerel, was it? What a terrible name for bad poetry. Now, if Wishbone had been thinking up a name for it, he could have come up with a much better one.

Catterel, for example.

Chapter Seven

Joe was breathing hard at the end of the long bike ride. Christy lived in a rambling gray-frame house with a yard full of tough, springy grass and pineapple palms. These were small palm trees, not much taller than Joe, with pear-shaped trunks that really did look like huge pineapples. Behind Christy's house was a canal, a narrow, straight waterway that fed into a river. The river emptied into the bay.

"Is that your catamaran?" Joe asked. He pointed toward a weathered old dock. On the grass beside it was a little blue-aluminum craft that looked to Joe about as seaworthy as a log raft.

"That's the *Suncatcher*," Christy said cheerfully. "I'm going to run inside and tell my grandmother where we'll be. Don't let Wishbone get too close to the canal."

"He can swim," Joe said.

Christy shook her head as she walked toward the house. "It isn't that, Joe. There may be an alligator around. Gators just love to snack on little dogs!"

"Alligators!" Joe said, feeling a bit stunned. "I guess we'd better stick close to the house until she gets back, Wishbone."

Several minutes passed, and Joe began to feel a little uneasy. He kept glancing at the canal. Then the door leading from the house banged open, and Christy came out. She was waving a folded piece of paper the size of a magazine page.

"Granny had a bright idea," Christy said. "We can do a little planning first. Come on."

Mystified, Joe followed her around to the side of the house. She led him to a picnic table beneath a strangely shaped oak tree, one that had grown leaning over to one side. Christy picked up four big conch shells—the large, pink, cone-shaped shells that had points sticking out on the wide end—and spread out the paper. She rested the shells on the corners to hold it down.

Coming up beside Christy, Joe saw that the paper was a map. It was printed in dark blue, and it showed the shoreline of St. George Bay. Dotted lines swirled through the water areas, with numbers marked on them. "Is this a navigation chart?" Joe asked.

"Yes. My dad does a little fishing and boating, and he's got a whole bunch of them. Now, let's see that poem."

Joe pulled it out of his pocket. "Here it is."

Wishbone leaped up onto the picnic-table bench, then up onto the table. He looked down at the map as if he, too, were curious.

Christy smoothed the paper. "Find the part that mentions Faith and Hope and read it out loud."

Joe found the place, cleared his throat, and began to read:

"Faith's a friend, and there begin,
And bear five points to starboard.
Pull hearty then, and pull to win,

Pull with all your might—
And with each pull, may my curse fall,
Devil take the keeper o' the Skeleton Reef Light!
Bear down ten, bear another five,
Hope for luck, and three and thirty;
Then larboard, seven and twenty strive.
'Tis gold, 'tis gold, ye seek for charity,
Three Sisters will guard it there for ye. . . ."

"Okay," said Christy. She had been putting smaller shells on the map to hold it down. "Take a look at this."

Joe looked on as she tapped a spot out in the bay. "Skeleton Reef Light, right?"

"Okay, I see it."

Wishbone took a step onto the map and began to sniff. Joe gently pulled him back. Christy moved her finger to a small island on the right side of the bay, near the spot where a river emptied into the Gulf. "Can you read the name of the island?"

Joe leaned forward and felt his heart thump. "Faith Island!"

"That's where you're supposed to begin, right? Now, *points* are directions, keyed to the compass. If you go five points to starboard, or right, you would wind up here." She moved her finger left.

"That's the wrong way," Joe protested.

"Only if you're looked at the map with north at the top. Pretend you're standing up in the lighthouse, looking out at the bay."

"Oh, I see."

Christy tapped the map. "Five points, and you'd wind up about here." She tapped the paper at the narrow end of a larger, pear-shaped island. "This is the west end of Hope Island." She sighed. "Trouble is, that's a dead end. The rest of the numbers don't make sense."

Joe took another look at the poem. "Charity is mentioned, too," he pointed out. "Faith, Hope, and Charity."

"And there is no Charity Island," Christy said.

For another half hour they puzzled over the map. No matter how they interpreted the strange numbers—as directions, as feet, yards, miles, or sea-miles (which are longer than land-miles)—they made no progress in figuring out the meaning in the poem.

At last Christy shrugged. "Well, we can always go visit the lighthouse, and maybe the nearby islands. Be back in a sec."

She put the shells back where they had come from—along the border of a flowerbed—and then expertly folded the big map. She ran inside, letting the door bang shut again.

A few minutes later, Christy came outside. A short, elderly Asian woman was with her. "Granny Lee, this is Joe. Joe, this is my grandmother. She started the first Lee's Restaurant in St. George Bay. Oh, and Granny, this is Wishbone."

"Very pleased to meet you," Granny Lee said, smiling. "Don't let this granddaughter of mine spill you into the bay!"

"I'll be careful," Joe promised.

Christy just rolled her eyes. "Come on. While I'm giving you some sailing lessons, you can tell me why the poem isn't just a load of garbage."

Christy, Joe, and Wishbone went to the dock. With a little shoving, they pushed the catamaran from the canal bank to the water. The craft was like a flat platform with low sides, resting on two long aluminum floats, or pontoons. A mast went into a socket in the forward part of the boat. From a locker on the old pier, Christy had taken two orange life vests and tossed one to Joe.

As Joe put on the life jacket, Christy untied the sail and explained what the different ropes were. "Call them *lines*," she advised, "because no sailor calls them *ropes*."

Soon Joe was sitting on a low seat, or thwart. Wishbone was beside him, looking alert and ready for adventure.

"Oh, we can't go yet," Christy said. "Every ship needs a captain." She whistled shrilly.

Joe looked toward the house. A shaggy orange form like a miniature—well, sort of miniature—lion was bounding across the lawn. "Don't tell me that cat is the captain! Won't the alligators get him?" Joe asked.

"Nope," Christy answered right away. "They're all afraid of him."

Joe held Wishbone as the cat ran onto the ram-shackle pier, leaped, and landed with a plop in the stern of the catamaran. Ignoring Wishbone's low growl, Cap'n Ahab took his time strolling forward. He curled up in front of the mast, in the bow of the vessel, and seemed to be ready for the trip.

"We'll paddle our way out to the river," Christy announced. She handed Joe one of two short wooden paddles. "There's no room for maneuvering in the canal."

Joe had a little trouble with his paddle. Soon, however, he got the knack. The catamaran glided through the dark, almost black, water of the canal. After about a quarter of a mile, the canal opened out, and then they were in the river. The water there was a muddy brown, and it emptied into St. George Bay. Joe could see the spreading brown stain of it flowing into the emerald-green waters of the Gulf.

Flocks of gray-white-and-black seagulls swooped low, shrieking at them. Wishbone barked a warning.

"Those are laughing gulls," Christy said. "They sound as if they're having fun, don't they?"

Listening to the high-pitched "Haa! Haa!—Haa! Haa!—Haa! Haa!" cries of the gulls, Joe thought they sounded more like a flock of chickens that had lost it. Three pelicans flew by, all in a straight line. The lead one flapped its big wings. The second reached the same spot, then flapped. The one at the rear of the line waited until it was in the exact same spot, and then it flapped, too. Their flight path was like a birdy game of "follow the leader."

To Joe, the big birds looked strange and prehistoric, like pterodactyls. As the sail began to catch the wind, Joe didn't have to paddle anymore. He relaxed and began to enjoy the trip.

Christy told Joe to hand her the paddle. She stowed it against one of the catamaran's low sides. "Okay," she said, showing Joe how to haul on a line so the sail swung around. "Now, tie that line off to the cleat—no, make a figure-eight, like this—there. Now I can steer, and you can tell me more about the poem."

She took the tiller. As the little sail filled with wind, the catamaran leaned to the side and began to skim forward. Joe grabbed one of the sides—Christy called them "gunwales"—and held on tight. He could hear the swift curl of water at the bows.

"You'll have to trim sail every once in a while," Christy warned Joe.

"Uh . . . trim it . . . how?" Joe asked.

Christy shook her head. "That means you have to pull either this line or that one to move the sail," she explained. "You have to keep the sail adjusted so the wind fills it and pushes us along. I'll show you which line to pull when it's time. Meanwhile, you can tell me all about this poem, and why you think you can figure it out when nobody else has been able to."

Wishbone was sitting close to Joe. He raised his head jauntily, appearing to enjoy the trip.

Joe reached into his shirt pocket and unfolded the paper. "I'm not sure that I *can* figure it out," he admitted. "It's like a mystery that I read, though."

He told Christy about "The Musgrave Ritual." He explained how Sherlock Holmes had solved the puzzle of a strange-sounding ceremony. Holmes realized that the ritual gave directions to something: "North by ten and by ten, east by five and by five, south by two and by two, west by one and by one, and so under," the ritual had read.

The problem was that no one could follow the odd directions. Joe told Christy how the old ritual was said to have begun under the shadow of an elm tree— only no elm tree existed, because it had been struck by lightning and was destroyed. Before Holmes could solve the puzzle, he first had to deduce where the elm tree had stood years ago.

"Sounds neat," Christy admitted. "Maybe I'd enjoy reading that story. Hugo Gilmore wasn't exactly Sherlock Holmes, though."

Joe nodded. "I know. Still, Carperdale knew Hugo Gilmore, and he doesn't think this poem's a hoax. People might take it more seriously if the original was still around."

"The *carved* one?"

"That's right."

Christy didn't say anything for a moment. Joe was thinking furiously. Sometimes in the Sherlock Holmes tales, one clue was no good all by itself, but it led to, or combined with, another piece of the puzzle. In "The Musgrave Ritual," for example, Holmes had to figure out that the directions were useless until someone looked for a hidden trapdoor.

The lighthouse. Was the lighthouse like that trapdoor? Was it the key to solving the mystery?

Just then Christy slid sideways at the tiller. "Okay, Joe, we're going to turn. When I tell you, I want you to pull on that line so the boom swings back and around. This is called 'coming about.' The first stage is to pull the line so the sail loses the wind. Do that when I say 'Prepare to come about,' okay?"

"Okay."

Christy moved the tiller, and the catamaran started to turn. "Prepare to come about!"

Joe hauled on the line until the sail fluttered.

"Now," said Christy, "when I say 'Helm's alee,' that means I've turned the boat so it's facing right into the wind. That's the tricky time. Then you have to pull the boom hard the other way, so the sail will catch the wind on the other side and take us in a new direction. Ready?"

"Ready."

Christy moved the tiller, and the little craft turned. "Helm's alee!"

Joe hauled the boom around, and the sail swung out to the left. The wind caught and filled it. Following Christy's instruction, Joe made the line fast to a cleat. "Was that okay?" he asked.

She grinned at him. "First-rate. We just came about. See where we are?"

Joe leaned over to look past the sail. The entire bay lay before them. Directly ahead, but still a long way off, was the Skeleton Reef Light. "Uh-oh," Joe said. "We ran into trouble out there yesterday morning with

a man named Nathaniel Bevans." Joe told her what had happened.

"I know him. He *is* sort of peculiar." Christy craned her neck to take a good look at the lighthouse. "Tell you what. We'll sail all the way around the lighthouse. If we don't see his little boat, then we'll know it's safe to land."

Wishbone barked.

Joe frowned at him. Cap'n Ahab raised his head to give Wishbone an angry shushing scowl.

"What is it, boy? Something about the lighthouse?"

Wishbone barked again.

"Maybe he's scared of old Nate the Nut," Christy said. "Or maybe he's trying to tell us something else."

"Maybe he's trying to tell us the lighthouse is the key to the whole mystery," Joe said.

Wishbone gave his best friend a grateful look.

"Come on," Christy said. "Who's going to listen to a dog?"

Wishbone sighed, as if he were all too familiar with that opinion.

Chapter Eight

The wind wasn't strong, and Christy's catamaran did a lazy sweep across the bay. The waves chopped at the little boat, but Joe did not suffer from seasickness. Wishbone appeared to feel fine, too. As for Cap'n Ahab, he lay curled up in the center of a white doughnut-shaped life preserver in the bow.

"There's Faith Island," Christy said. "We may as well take a look at that first." The catamaran leaned with the wind as they changed direction again.

They passed by the island at a distance of about thirty yards—around one-third the length of a football field. Joe strained his eyes. All he could see, however, was a confusion of reedy plants, a few glimpses of white sand, and dozens of gray gulls and white egrets. He also spotted a flock of white terns with jet-black caps wading, hovering, landing, or taking off.

"Does anybody live there?" Joe asked.

"Are you kidding?" Christy replied with a laugh. "It's barely more than a mud flat. I'll bet the bugs would eat you alive if you landed. The birds would be pretty upset, too!"

The catamaran leaned as they turned again, this

time in a different way that Christy called a *jibe*. That meant Joe had to move the sail so it would catch the wind on the left side instead of the right, but Christy didn't turn the boat into the wind. It was a more gradual change of direction than coming about was.

Then, out on the open bay, they caught a better breeze and skimmed along the water. The lighthouse grew steadily larger as Christy steered toward it.

They sailed around the lighthouse reef. Then Christy announced that the coast was clear. "It's a good day for fishing," she said. "Nate has probably hired himself out as a guide and has some tourists over in the grass flats, fishing for bonefish or snook." She explained that grass flats were marshy, reed-filled places. They were good fishing spots.

Christy turned the *Suncatcher* again. They laboriously tacked back against the wind, making sideways, zigzagging progress. At last Christy told Joe to get ready. They came up alongside the concrete base of the lighthouse. Joe dropped the sail, and moments later Christy jumped off the catamaran and tied a line to a cleat. Joe passed her a second line. A few minutes after that, Christy, Joe, and Wishbone stood at the base of the lighthouse. Cap'n Ahab jumped out all by himself and glared around as if dissatisfied.

The tide was low. At the side of the lighthouse, a jumbled, shell-filled island wallowed, barely above the waterline. Christy tugged experimentally at the rusty metal door of the lighthouse. It creaked on its hinges as it swung open heavily. "It isn't kept locked?" Joe asked.

"It doesn't even have a lock anymore," Christy told him. "What's the point? There's nothing to steal!" She picked up shaggy Cap'n Ahab. "I'm going inside, yes, I am," she said in a baby-like voice. "Big, brave

83

Cap'n Ahab has to stay and guard the *Suncatcher*, yes he does."

Joe rolled his eyes. He was glad he didn't make that sort of fuss over Wishbone, who was glaring at the cat as if disgusted. Joe was happy, too, that the cat would be staying behind. That meant he wouldn't have to hold Wishbone's collar every moment.

Joe gasped for air as soon as they stepped inside the lighthouse tower. The air was humid and hot, and he began to sweat. The only light came from what filtered through the four side windows, high up in the walls, and they were smeared with a salt glaze. In the center of the tower, an open spiral staircase, made of what looked like rusty iron, wound up into the gloom. Frayed old electric wires ran up the brick walls. Running right up through the center of the spiral staircase, a cluster of three rusty pipes led up into the dimness. The top of the staircase was dark.

"Be careful," Christy warned. "Maybe I'd better go first."

"No," Joe said. "Let me go up first."

However, neither led the way, because Wishbone darted ahead.

They climbed the staircase slowly. It screeched and groaned alarmingly under their weight. The heat grew even worse as they climbed. It was a suffocating, muggy heat, and it clogged Joe's lungs. The place smelled musty and damp. The stairs seemed to wind on forever.

When they reached the level of the windows, Joe stared out. But years and years of drying salt had become encrusted on the windows, making them translucent instead of transparent. It was like trying to look through waxed paper. All he could see was a bright blue blur, sea and sky blending into each other.

After more climbing, at last they emerged at the level of the glassed-in lamp chamber. Joe took some deep breaths. The air was much better there, cooler and less muggy. An enormous light stood in the center. Its lens was made of greenish glass cast in concentric circles. The diameter of the lens was at least four feet. The light rested on an arrangement of gears that once had turned it around and around, directing its beam out at sea to guide incoming ships. Now, Joe saw, the gears were so rusty they probably could not even move.

A glass door opened onto a narrow windowed gallery. A rusted iron railing surrounded the platform. Christy shoved the door open—the old frame was warped and stuck—and she and Joe took a single careful step out.

Joe caught his breath. "You'd better stay inside, Wishbone, and guard the steps."

Wishbone's tail wagged.

Joe pulled the door almost closed. He and Christy were so high up that he felt dizzy. Fifty feet below them, the bay glistened. Parts of it were deep turquoise. In other places, where the water was shallow, the colors changed to pale green, yellow, or even brown. Christy explained that the brown patches were where lots of Gulf weed had collected.

Christy walked around, with Joe following close behind her, gripping the railing. The shore spread out like a tiny toy town in a model-railroad setup. He pointed to a distant house. "That's Rhonda's place," he said.

"Right. And over there is Faith Island. Out past it is Hope. Hmm . . ."

"What is it?" Joe asked.

Christy shook her head. "I was just thinking. Here's the lighthouse, and there are two of the places named in Hugo's poem. Maybe the numbers aren't paces or rods or furlongs or miles or any other kind of distance measure. They just might be bearings."

"Bearings? What do you mean, bearings?"

"Measurements of angles," Christy explained. "It's like trigonometry in school. . . . Would you mind hanging out here for a few minutes? I want to go back to the boat for something."

"I think I'll wait inside. Wishbone might get lonely."

Christy made her way into the main section of the lighthouse and descended the stairs.

Joe stood there for a minute or two. He was beginning to feel a little less queasy about being up so high. The walkway he stood on was solid, and the railing, although rusty, had been firmly mortared into place. He looked down again. Way down below he could see the blue catamaran, almost directly under the lighthouse. Other boats dotted the bay. Some speedboats sped along, creating V-shaped wakes of white water behind them.

Joe went back inside and lifted Wishbone up so his pal could see the view. The glass in the lamp chamber was much cleaner than what was in the other windows.

Joe said, "Maybe somebody keeps it neat up here. The lens has been polished. I guess that must be Mr. Bevans's work."

Wishbone licked his buddy's chin. Joe laughed and set him down. Steps creaked on the spiral staircase. In a moment Christy stepped out into the light chamber. She carried with her a metal instrument. "Here we go."

"What's that?"

"A sextant. Sailors use these to get bearings. If I'm right, it might help us solve the puzzle."

86

Christy and Joe went back out onto the walk again. Wishbone stayed put. Christy showed Joe how the sextant worked. She chose two distant spots and sighted along the sextant. She used a compass to figure directions. However, after a few moments of trying, she sighed and shook her head. "It's not working."

"Maybe you're not doing it right."

She gave him a cool look. "I know math and navigation. I have an A-plus average in math at school, and I take the accelerated courses. I can do plane and spherical geometry and trigonometry. With a sextant, a good watch, and a compass, I can plot my location and set a course anywhere in the world. I'm not bragging. I'm telling you that if I can't line up the landmarks like Faith and Hope islands, nobody else can. Okay?"

Joe could not help smiling. "Okay, okay. Sorry."

"It's all right. You didn't know." She sighed. "Rats. For a second there, I thought I had something. I guess

Brad Strickland and Thomas E. Fuller

someone else would have tried that over the years, though. I'm sure that even Nathaniel Bevans would have thought of it."

Joe sighed. "Sherlock Holmes had it easy in 'The Musgrave Ritual.' He cracked the mystery when he realized the elm tree that was mentioned as the starting point no longer existed. He used trigonometry to figure out where its shadow would be, though, and that solved his problem."

Christy shrugged. "It looks as if our mystery is going to be harder to solve."

They went back into the light chamber. Joe was feeling very discouraged.

Wishbone's excellent sense of hearing had allowed him to listen to every word that Joe and Christy had said. His tail drooped as his friend came back inside.

"Bummer, Joe. I really thought you had something. I guess you'll just have to try again." He perked up. "Fortunately, you have one of the great minds of our century helping you. I'd tell you whose it is, but I happen to be very modest!"

"I don't think we should give up," Joe said.

Christy snorted. "Who said anything about giving up? Look, if finding the treasure was as easy as that, it would have been found already, right?"

Wishbone nodded. "Smart thinking, Christy. How could someone as intelligent as you hang out with a cat?"

"You're right," Joe said. "Hmm . . . In the Sherlock Holmes story, everything depended on Holmes's deciding how the *original* directions worked. You know, maybe the problem is with the copy of the poem. I mean, Hugo was only ten when he made it. What if he didn't get all the words or numbers right?"

Wishbone yipped. "Right! Just one small error could put you a long way off the trail! It's like the times when I can't remember whether I've buried my chew toy in Wanda's petunias or in her black-eyed Susans!"

Christy sounded thoughtful when she said, "The only way to check that would be to find the original wooden bed frame."

"That's the problem." Joe squinted. Watching him, Wishbone felt a growing sense of excitement. He could tell that Joe was getting an idea. Joe said slowly, "I wonder if that old wooden bed was just a platform, like a little table."

"It was," Christy said promptly.

"How do you know that?" Joe asked.

"A couple of them still exist," Christy said. "We have one in the foyer of our restaurant. It's an antique. It's just three old splintery boards, each one about six-teen inches wide and six and a half feet long. Dad built a platform with legs for it, so we could use it as a table. It holds menus and brochures about things to do in the bay area. But it *doesn't* have any carving on the under-side, or we would have noticed!"

Wishbone looked up into Joe's face. "Hear that, Joe? Are you thinking what I'm thinking?"

Joe grinned. "What if someone took one of those apart?" he asked. "What would you have then?"

Christy shrugged. "Just three long boards, two supporting timbers, and three cross-pieces. Why?"

"In 'The Musgrave Ritual,'" Joe said slowly, "there's a trapdoor. Only no one knows it's a trapdoor, because it's made of stone. It's in the middle of a floor made of identical paving stones. Maybe the bed has been hidden in a place just as obvious. I think I need to get back to Rhonda's. There's something I have to check."

"What is it?"

Joe shook his head. "I'll explain later. It may not be anything at all. If it isn't, I don't want to look goofy."

They went down the spiral staircase, back down through the gloom and heat of the lighthouse tower. Joe gave the old door a push. It groaned open on its rusty hinges, and the trio stepped outside. Wishbone squinted in the bright sunlight.

"Let's find Cap'n Ahab," Christy said.

They found him out at the edge of the oyster-shell island. He was stalking small white crabs. The cat would crouch down, freeze, then dart forward as an unlucky crab came within its striking range. Then Cap'n Ahab would give a tremendous swipe with his paw, and he would bat the crab out into the bay. Sometimes he hit one so hard that it skipped once or twice before sinking.

Just like a cat, Wishbone thought.

Christy gathered up Cap'n Ahab into her arms. Then the whole group got back aboard the catamaran. They sailed back to the river on a gusty inshore breeze. Behind them in the Gulf, clouds were building up on the horizon. The shore ahead looked peaceful and cheerful enough, but that was the only sign of cheer.

Great, Wishbone thought, yawning. *We went out there expecting to find Ben Walker's treasure. But all we got out of the trip was tired.* Trusting Joe to keep watch on the monster cat up in the bow, Wishbone settled down for a nap.

Chapter Nine

"What have you got up your sleeve?" Christy asked Joe as they rode the tandem bike up the drive in front of Gilmore's Rest. Wishbone hopped out of the basket, shook himself, and dashed up onto the porch. When Christy got off the bike, the flap of her backpack opened and Cap'n Ahab stuck his head out. After one lazy glance around, he curled up inside the backpack again.

Joe parked the bike. "I have an idea. There may be nothing to it, but then again, you never know. Sometimes clues are too obvious. Look, if you had something made of boards and you wanted to hide it, what would you do?"

"Make a table out of it."

"Only that wouldn't be any good, because it would be too easy to see the carving if it was on the top. And you might see the carving on the underside of the table if you moved it. So what else could you do?"

"Build a doghouse. Turn it into a planter. Make a raft . . . I give up."

They went up the steps and Joe opened the door. They entered the cool foyer. "Or, take the bed frame apart and use the boards somewhere special—a place where the carving could be covered up by something that was put on the boards."

"Wallpaper," Christy said, following Joe through the house. "Plaster." They stepped through a doorway and into the study. Christy started to say something, blinked twice, then said softly, "Oh . . . Books! Absolutely brilliant, my dear Holmes!"

"Maybe," Joe said, looking at the shelves full of books. "I think I'd better find Carperdale."

The caretaker was upstairs, supervising the painters. They were putting the finishing touches on the last room to be painted on the second floor.

Carperdale listened to what Joe had to say. Then he whistled. "By Jove, Joseph, you may have something. I'll be right down—and I shall bring a ladder!"

Joe, Christy, and Wishbone went back downstairs to wait.

Carperdale was downstairs in the study with them in a couple of minutes, carrying a stepladder. However, once there, he shook his head. "Dear me. I should say these shelves are too short to serve as a bed."

"Maybe," Joe said. "But if you hadn't yet cut them in half, though—"

"I see what you mean." Carperdale looked thoughtful. "Mr. Hugo always said that his father resented the publicity his discovery brought. The old man confiscated the bed, and Mr. Hugo never knew what happened to it. I suppose there is a chance the carving is here. Where shall we begin, then?"

Wishbone barked, pointing with his nose. Joe laughed. "I agree with Wishbone. I think these old records of commercial fishing probably haven't been read in years."

Carperdale nodded, his eyes gleaming. "Quite

right! I've kept them dusted, but I've never looked inside them. Nor has anyone else, as far as I know. Here goes nothing!"

He climbed onto the ladder and began to remove books from the top shelf, near the ceiling. He handed them down to Joe and Christy. They stacked them neatly on the floor. When the shelf was empty, Carperdale carefully pulled it off its supports. "Heavy," he muttered. He climbed down with it, stared at it, and set it down triumphantly on the floor.

"Joe!" Christy gasped. "You did it!"

Joe swelled with pride. His guess had been a good one, all right. Part of the poem—the middle part of the first twenty lines or so—was clearly visible, carved into the old wood. Above that was a crude carving of a lighthouse.

"This is really it," Joe said.

"Indeed, Joseph!" Carperdale said, clapping him on the shoulder. "A feat worthy of Her Majesty's Secret Service!" He coughed and then said, "Do forgive me, Joseph. I spent some years in the Royal Navy dealing with those intelligence chaps, and this exploit reminded me of that time."

"Don't apologize," Joe said happily. "Let's just dig out the other shelves!"

Half an hour later, they had assembled the whole bed frame on the floor, like a jigsaw puzzle with only six pieces to it. It was a little more than three and a half feet wide, and about six and a half feet long.

Carperdale pointed at holes drilled through the edge of two of the boards. "This was where the chains were fastened," he explained. "One edge of the bed was

93

mortared into the cell wall. This edge had chains at the foot and the head, and the chains were attached to iron hooks in the walls. The platform would not have been easily removed. Ben Walker must have lain on the floor beneath it and carved the poem there with some small piece of metal. Perhaps he used even a little fragment of broken glass or pottery that would be easily concealed. He would not have been trusted to have a knife with him in his cell."

Joe unfolded his copy of Hugo's poem. He read it through word by word, comparing it with the carved version. Christy asked anxiously, "Is it different?"

Joe shook his head. "No. Just the same."

Wishbone's ears drooped.

"What in the world?"

Joe, Christy, and Carperdale turned around at the sound of Rhonda's voice. She was standing in the doorway, blinking at them in amazement.

Carperdale stepped forward. "Joseph has made a rather remarkable discovery," he said. He went on to explain what they had found.

Rhonda immediately called Wanda and Ellen in. They crowded around, looking at the strangely shaped, old-fashioned letters carved into the wood.

"Do you suppose it's valuable?" Wanda asked hopefully.

Rhonda snorted. "Oh, some collector would probably pay something for it. I don't think anyone would be crazy enough to offer $250,000 for a sample of old Ben Walker's handwriting—or hand-carving, I suppose, is more like it."

"Then I don't see how it helps us." Wanda shook her head and sighed. "For just a moment there, I'd hoped— Oh, Joe, you tried your best."

"I think Joe had a great idea," Christy said loyally.

Ellen looked down at the carving. "Is it exactly the same as Hugo's copy, Joe?"

To make sure, Rhonda brought the old notebook in. They went over the poem again, line by line. Wishbone sniffed at the top edge of the carving. Joe felt a sense of rising disappointment as they came to the last refrain of "Devil take the keeper o' the Skeleton Reef Light." He said, "It's exactly the same."

Wishbone barked, pawing at the carving of the lighthouse.

Ellen patted her son's shoulder. "Christy is right, Joe. Your idea was great. It was very smart of you to find it. That was good thinking."

"Thanks, Mom, but I was hoping— You know, every time I think I have something figured out about this poem, I turn out to be all wrong." Joe told them about the trip out to the lighthouse he and Christy had made. He explained how he had guessed where the old bed might be.

Wishbone yipped again. He pawed the top of the middle board.

Wanda gave Joe a weak smile. "I do appreciate your trying to help, Joe. But I got myself and the Oakdale Historical Society into this mess, so I suppose it's up to me to get us out—if I can."

Ellen asked, "What did the commissioners say? Will they at least give you more time?"

"No," Wanda answered. "They were polite, but they say they've already waited too long. So, either the old lighthouse has to be repaired and the base reinforced so it won't fall over in a storm, or else it has to be torn down. They said the situation would be different if it were really a historical site, but it's just an old lighthouse, like dozens of others."

Joe's heart sank. "That's not true! This lighthouse *is* special."

Christy chimed in. "Joe's right. The Skeleton Reef Light has lots of history behind it. It was tied in with the wreck of the *Mad Mary's Revenge*. The pirate Ben Walker was captured in a small boat out close to it. He was supposed to be just as fierce as Blackbeard, and everyone knows about Blackbeard."

Rhonda said, "Unfortunately, I suppose the commission doesn't feel those are very important historical events. Sometimes it really does seem as if the Skeleton Reef Light has a curse hanging over it. It's had a lot of bad luck over the years. There was the shipwreck back in the 1700s. Then came the big hurricane in the early 1800s that wiped out a lot of the town and blew away the first lighthouse keepers' cottage. After that was the explosion during the Civil War, when the Confederates—"

"Explosion!" Joe exclaimed. "That's right! You told me about that! How did it damage the lighthouse?"

Rhonda shrugged. "It blew up part of the tower. I think the Confederates blasted off the top twenty feet or so."

Joe thought hard. "Then the lighthouse is *shorter* than it used to be?"

Rhonda said, "No, because after the Civil War ended, the lighthouse was rebuilt. The island it stands on now was higher then. It was out of the water all the time. The crew that rebuilt the lighthouse added a new keeper's cottage, a new fuel house—in the old days, the light was actually an oil lantern, not an electric light—and repaired the tower. By the time they finished, the new lighthouse was about twenty feet taller than the old one. The old one's light was about forty feet above the water, and the new one is exactly sixty feet up."

Wishbone pawed at Joe's leg. He looked down at

his pal. Then he gazed at the carved picture of the lighthouse. "Then maybe that isn't just a bad carving," Joe said. "Maybe that's the way the lighthouse really looked in Captain Ben Walker's day."

Wishbone wagged his tail.

For a few moments they all stared at the carved picture of the lighthouse. It seemed to be shorter than the modern-day lighthouse in the bay. There were only the small round windows in the tower. The top was different, too, with a roof that seemed flatter and broader than the present one.

"It's interesting," Rhonda said, "but not really historical."

"I don't know," Christy said slowly. "It's pretty confusing."

Joe asked, "Could we go out again tomorrow on your catamaran?"

"Well . . . sure," Christy said. "My dad won't mind, if it's okay with your mom."

"Please, Mom?" asked Joe.

Ellen smiled. "If you're careful and wear your life jacket."

"I will."

Christy said, "I've got to go now, but I'll be over bright and early tomorrow. Hey, where's Cap'n Ahab?" She had picked up her backpack and had discovered that it was empty.

"We'll help you find him," Joe said.

The second that Wishbone heard Cap'n Ahab was missing, he got a very bad feeling. He dashed into the kitchen, and his worst fears had come true. His dry-food bowl was empty!

Sitting next to it, calmly licking himself, was the greedy cat culprit. Wishbone growled. "Look, you mangy pirate cat, this port isn't big enough for the two of us!"

Cap'n Ahab ignored him. He found one tiny piece of dry food on the floor, crunched it, and swallowed it. Then he began to purr.

"Ohh—just wait till I bark for Joe! Are you going to get it!" Wishbone barked, and a moment later Joe and Christy came into the kitchen.

"There you are," Christy said, scooping up the cat. "You're a bad boy, yes, you are, to scare me like that."

Wishbone shook his head. "Can I believe my ears? You're not going to punish that creature?"

"See you tomorrow," Christy said, stuffing Cap'n Ahab into her backpack.

"See you," Joe said.

Wishbone waited until Christy had left the house. Then he picked up his empty food bowl in his mouth and stared up at Joe. He gave his pal the great-big-sad-puppy-eyes routine. "See whaff thaff cath did foo me? He ftole all my food!"

"No more, Wishbone," Joe said. He took the bowl and set it down. "You're eating too much. You don't want to get fat."

Wishbone could only stare at Joe. "Fat! Me? *I'm* not fat! The cat is fat! And I wish he were flat! Splat! A fat, fat cat, flat as a mat!" The Jack Russell shook his head. "Whoa! I'm so upset, I'm slipping back into puppy talk! I'll find some way to pay back that thieving feline, mark my words. As Joe is my witness, that cat will never make me go hungry again!"

Late that night a storm came in off the Gulf. Wind-whipped rain pounded against Joe's bedroom window. He got up and opened the blind. Lightning flashed. In the sudden, brief light, he caught a glimpse of the churning water. There were waves capped with white, and sheets of rain lashing in from the Gulf. The house shook from the booming thunder. Wishbone shivered. He stood up on the foot of the bed and pressed his head against Joe's leg.

"It's okay, boy," Joe said, as another bolt of lightning turned night into day. "It's just a little storm."

Wishbone snuffled.

"Hey!" Joe said. "There's a light on in the lighthouse." He leaned close to the window, his forehead pressed against the cool, hard glass. Squinting into the darkness, he could see a faint yellow light showing in the light chamber. It wasn't the blaze of the lighthouse lamp, but a soft glow, as if someone was in the lighthouse with a kerosene lantern.

Joe padded out of his room, barefoot, and went

downstairs to the study. On one of the shelves there he found Hugo Gilmore's old brass spyglass. It was the one that Rhonda had said the old man had used to watch ships. Joe borrowed it and returned to his room. He raised his window, flinching as some cold rain spat in. Steadying the spyglass on the windowsill, Joe looked at the top of the lighthouse.

There was no doubt about it—someone *did* have a lantern up there. As he stared, Joe saw a figure pacing around on the walk outside the light chamber. Just then a bolt of lightning lit everything up, and Joe gasped.

Pacing around the walk, ignoring the storm, his own telescope gripped in his hands, was the grim figure of Nathaniel Bevans, haunting the lighthouse even in dangerous weather.

Like a ghost, Joe thought. *Just like a ghost.*

Chapter Ten

"I don't know," Christy said slowly. She looked up at the morning sky. It was filled with racing, ragged gray clouds. "The weather looks chancy."

Joe spread his hands in frustration. "Just long enough to check! Sherlock Holmes would go take a look!"

Christy shook her head. "Explain to me exactly what all this means, Sherlock."

Joe felt a growing assurance that he had guessed right. "It's simple. The old lighthouse was shorter than this one. Somehow or other, Captain Walker did a survey from the top of the lighthouse tower back in 1765. He wrote down bearings that would lead to his ship. In 1922, though, when Hugo found the poem, the tower was twenty feet taller." Joe could not keep his voice from growing more excited. "That means the bearings are off. Now, if we adjust the measurements for the higher tower—"

Christy's brown eyes widened. "I see. If we adjust for the difference, we'd be able to find the spot the poem names! That's brilliant, Joe!"

Joe laughed modestly and said, "Elementary, my dear Watson!"

About Thomas E. Fuller

THOMAS E. FULLER has always loved writing and dogs. So when the opportunity arose to write about a dog—and that dog just happened to be the one and only Wishbone—he jumped at the chance to co-author *The Treasure of Skeleton Reef* with his friend Brad Strickland. Thomas came up with the idea for the pirate Ben Walker, whose career was based on that of the real pirate Edward Teach, better known as "Blackbeard." Like Ben Walker, Blackbeard really destroyed his ship, the *Queen Anne's Revenge*, to keep his men from sharing his loot!

Thomas has written and published adult short stories and novelettes, but this is his first book for young readers. He is best known as the author of twenty original plays and more than forty audio dramas, as the head writer of the Atlanta Radio Theatre Company (ARTC). His adaptation of H. G. Wells's *The Island of Dr. Moreau* recently won the Silver Mark Tyme Award for Best Science Fiction Audio of 1996. Thomas is also writing a young-adult novel with his artist wife, Berta. Currently, he and Brad Strickland are working on the new Wishbone audio series. They are also finishing their next Wishbone Mystery title, *The Riddle of the Wayward Books*.

When Thomas isn't writing, he works at a Barnes & Noble bookstore, teaches creative writing, and acts with ARTC. He and Berta have four children—Edward, Anthony, John, and Christina. They share a very cluttered house in Duluth, Georgia, with a large collection of books and audio tapes, stacks of manuscripts and paintings, and all the children in the neighborhood. Their special housemate is a gigantic twenty-pound orange cat, The General, who served as the model for Captain Ahab.

Now Playing on Your VCR...

The two were standing in the backyard of Gilmore's Rest. The lawn sloped away, ending in a tangle of spiky-leafed palmettos and tall, grassy sea oats. The palm fronds rattled and the sea oats bounced and swayed in the wind. Beyond the dunes lay the Gulf, out of sight. The southern horizon seemed strangely cut off—gray, dim, and misty. Cap'n Ahab prowled around the yard, sniffing at this and that. He crept about with high, dainty cat steps, and Wishbone watched him alertly.

After the rough, noisy night, the weather had improved. At least it was no longer storming, although beads of rain still glistened on the broad fans of the palm tops. More droplets glittered like jewels in the tangled gray beards of Spanish moss hanging from the wind-twisted live-oak trees. The storm had cooled the air.

Joe took a deep breath. "We have to try," he said. "It means a lot to everyone here in the town." He was wearing jeans, sandals, a short-sleeved shirt, and a blue baseball cap. The wind flapped his shirttail and tried to tug the cap right off his head. He clapped a hand down on it.

Christy, holding on to her own red cap, bit her lip. "You see how the weather is. The wind's from the southeast and pretty gusty. The water's got a rough chop this morning. Sailing out in a little catamaran would be tricky."

"I won't be in St. George Bay much longer," Joe pointed out. "We have to go back to Oakdale at the beginning of next week. Wishbone and I helped start all this. We'd like to finish it—or at least we'd like to *try* to finish it."

After a few moments, Christy nodded. "Okay. I've been out in worse weather, I guess. Come down here."

Following Christy across the yard to the dunes, Joe asked, "Where are we going?"

"Just to a place where we can see the bay." She climbed one of the dunes, with Joe right behind her. At the top she stood and pointed. "See the jetty there?"

Joe shaded his eyes. "Where all the boats are parked?"

Christy laughed. "You landlubber! You don't *park* a boat—you *moor* it. Anyway, walk over to where all those boats are moored. Then go out to the end of the pier. I'll be there about the same time you get there. If I were you, I'd just go down and stroll out along the beach."

"Okay."

"Take it easy. You don't really need to walk that fast. I'll meet you there at the end of the pier in about forty-five minutes."

Christy climbed on her bike and pedaled away. Joe and Wishbone went down to the beach. Dogs weren't allowed out on the public beach, but they were welcome back along the low, sandy dunes. Joe and Wishbone walked in the dunes, looking out at the gray-green Gulf.

As Christy had warned, the water was choppy, with lots of whitecaps. No families played in the surf this morning. Gulls soared and screeched, and pelicans sailed along in solemn formations. Wishbone kept finding things to sniff—broken seashells, pieces of driftwood, golf-ball-sized holes in the dunes that were ghost-crab burrows.

The wind kept gusting. By the time Joe and Wishbone reached the pier, it was scooping bursts of spray from the sharp crests of the waves. Wishbone shivered as he looked out over the water.

Joe petted him. "Looks rough, boy. I hope Christy's a good sailor!"

104

The catamaran was already heading toward the pier. Joe and Wishbone had to wait only a few moments before Christy came close enough to toss a line. Joe looped it around a piling, one of the telephone-pole-thick supports that held up the pier. Christy pulled in as close as she could. She was keeping low. In the bow, Cap'n Ahab was curled up in the center of his life ring.

"Okay," Christy said, sounding anxious. "Let Wishbone come aboard first."

That was easy enough, but then Joe had to step down into the boat. Christy told him to wait while she balanced the craft. She moved to the opposite side and leaned back. "Now!"

It was a difficult, long step. For a moment, Joe thought he was going to pitch overboard into the water. Then Christy leaned even farther, and he scrambled aboard. A sudden, cold wave broke against the catamaran's left pontoon, splashing Joe's arm and leg. "Rough!" he gasped.

"I've seen it rougher. Get ready—I'm casting off. "

Christy let Joe work the sail again. Fortunately, the catamaran had a very simple sail. Joe had only four lines to tug on or to release in order to control it. He tried hard to do everything Christy told him to do, almost as fast as she could say it. The sail had not been hauled all the way to the top of the mast, and Joe asked why.

"It's too windy," Christy said. "See how the bottom of the sail is tied to the boom?"

"The boom is the rod that keeps the bottom of the sail straight?" Joe asked.

"Right. See how the sail is tied to it? That's called 'reefing.' The wind would blow us sideways if the sail were all the way up. Reefing it lets us handle the gusts without tipping over."

It was a difficult, wet, uncomfortable run out to

the lighthouse, with gusting crosswinds coming from all directions. At last, though, they came close enough to the reef for Joe to clamber out hastily onto the concrete base. He caught the line Christy tossed to him and wound it around a cleat. The tide was higher than it had been on their last trip out. The rounded oyster reef was almost underwater. Rolling green waves burst into white spray as they broke in the shallows around the reef. Spray splashed up like heavy drizzle, making Joe's lips taste salty.

Christy adjusted the way the catamaran was tied. Then she, Cap'n Ahab, and Wishbone hopped ashore. Again, Cap'n Ahab remained outside. But he moved to the shelter of the lighthouse to avoid being hit by the spray. The other three got the rusty lighthouse door open and then entered. Then it slammed shut behind them. They stood for a moment in the darkness, letting their eyes adjust.

"At least it's cooler than last time," Joe said, his voice echoing loudly. The thick old brick walls kept out most of the wind's roar.

"But it's drafty," Christy said, shivering.

She was right. Even with the outer door closed, a stream of air rushed in and circled. In his wet clothes, Joe felt cold, too. "We'll be all right as soon as we start moving." Taking the lead, he began to climb the spiral staircase again.

Halfway up, Joe paused and pointed. "Look at that. It's obvious when you know what to look for."

"What?" asked Christy, sounding puzzled.

"Just about halfway up the bottom windows. Look at the bricks," Joe said. The two tall windows let in enough murky light to make it plain, he thought.

For a moment, Christy was quiet. Then Joe heard her gasp. "Oh. Now I see it."

106

Joe nodded. An uneven line ran all the way around the inside of the tower. Below it, the gray bricks were pitted with age, darker and rougher, stained with soot and with the passage of time. All the bricks above the line were whiter, smoother, and less worn.

Joe said, "That's the line where the repair work started when the lighthouse was rebuilt after the Civil War. Everything above that line is newer."

Wishbone climbed up a few steps, as if to see better. He led the way up the spiral staircase to the light chamber again. Christy had brought along her navigational instruments and a small spiral-bound pad. With a mechanical pencil, she began to make calculations. She rested the pad on a windowsill and penciled notes across it. Her pink tongue stuck out from the corner of her mouth as she concentrated.

At last she nodded, checked one last figure, then

looked at Joe with a nervous smile. "Okay. I think I can do it. Let's go. Be careful out there, though. It's wet and windy. It would be just great if we fell off and broke our necks."

Wishbone stayed inside as Joe and Christy went out onto the walk, where the whipping gusts made Joe clench his hands on the railing. Christy began to take sightings, while Joe looked up at the ragged, rushing clouds in the sky and worried.

Was it his imagination, or were the clouds getting thicker, darker? Was that dark gray curtain off to the southeast a heavy fall of rain out on the Gulf, getting closer at every moment? Was the occasional booming grumble he heard only the wind, or was it a distant roar of thunder?

Were they about to be caught in a raging storm?

When Joe and Christy left Wishbone alone in the light chamber, he felt tense. Something was coming— something unpleasant. The problem was that he had no idea what it could be. The air had a thundery smell, full of rain and wind and lightning. Wishbone paced, his nose twitching, his heart pounding faster than normal. How could he protect Joe if he didn't even know what the threat was?

Wishbone trotted round and round, wishing he were tall enough to look outside. He scratched at the door that led out onto the walkway. No use. It was closed tight. He stood on his hind legs, stretched up as far as he could, and discovered he could just see the narrow walk. The railing looked frail and rusty to him. The bricks on the walk glistened with water. "Be careful out there, Joe! Hold on tight! Watch your step!"

He dropped back to all fours and resumed his pacing. Trying to reassure himself, Wishbone thought with pride of how smart Joe had been. His buddy had realized the importance of the carved lighthouse after Wishbone had drawn his attention to it only three times. That was the great thing about humans. If a dog had patience, they could be taught— What was that? Wishbone's ears twitched at every hiss of wind. Something was building, all right.

What's about to happen? Wishbone asked himself. *My doggy sixth sense is trying to tell me something—but what?* Nervously, he licked his nose and glanced around the round room. He felt the skin on his neck crinkle as the hairs bristled. Everything inside him was trying to warn him of danger.

He was so edgy that when the door opened and Christy and Joe came in, Wishbone actually felt startled. They looked downcast.

"Rats!" Christy muttered. "If everything the poem says is right, the treasure should be buried just off the shore of Hope Island, not on the mainland."

"Well, it was worth a try," Joe said.

Christy shook her head. "Maybe I did the math wrong. If it was right, the treasure would be buried up on the mainland, smack in the middle of the Municipal Gardens. The trouble is, according to the poem, the place should be right off the coast of Hope."

Despite his worry, Wishbone had a moment when it was almost as though a light turned on inside his head. *"The Musgrave Ritual,"* he thought. *Look at the world in a different way! See how time can change things!*

He barked, trying to attract Joe's and Christy's attention.

Just at that moment, steps clanged on the spiral staircase—heavy, running steps.

109

Christy gasped.

Wishbone crouched.

Nathaniel Bevans, his gray hair wild, his eyes wide and glaring, burst inside. The thickset man wore a blue pea jacket, jeans, a black T-shirt, and heavy work boots. A gray frost of beard glittered on his chin. His chest was heaving as he gasped for breath.

For a moment, everyone froze in place. Then the stocky man glared at the others. "I warned ye!" he shouted. "I warned ye once, and ye wouldn't listen! . . . Doom! Doom has come for ye!"

Chapter Eleven

"**W**ishbone! No!"

Only Joe's loud command kept Wishbone from springing. Christy and Joe backed away from the strange man. His eyes seemed to bore right into them. Then he started to pace in the small area, waving his arms.

"Can't let a man alone, can ye?" Bevans said, his eyes bulging. "Got t' go where you're not s'posed to be! Well, I don't like people trespassin', see?" He stepped ever closer to the terrified trio, and Wishbone growled.

Anything could have happened at that moment. What *did* happen was that an orange blur sped through the doorway. With amazing accuracy, it wound up right between Mr. Bevans's feet. Cap'n Ahab let out a bloodcurdling screech as Bevans stumbled and lurched, waving his arms for balance.

"Run!" yelled Joe.

He and Christy dashed down the spiral staircase. Wishbone was close behind, running as fast as four legs could carry him. Even so, Cap'n Ahab passed them, going about fifty cat-miles per hour. From above, Joe could hear Mr. Bevans bellowing in anger.

"Quick!" Joe was holding the main door open. Wishbone zipped through in a heartbeat and leaped down into the catamaran without any help. In a moment, Joe was aboard, too. Christy and Cap'n Ahab were already there. As Joe fumbled with the mooring lines, he could hear the heavy clangs of Mr. Bevans's boots smacking the iron stairs as he hurried down in pursuit of them. "There!" Joe shouted, tossing the stern line aboard. "Let's go!"

He shoved against the concrete, and the catamaran swung free and caught the wind. The sudden lurch almost made Joe fall, but he caught himself just in time. Wishbone helpfully grabbed Joe's jeans leg in his teeth and held on tight.

In a second they were skimming across the choppy water. Thunder boomed behind them. Joe, holding tight to Wishbone, took a look back. The metal entrance door of the lighthouse banged open. Bevans charged outside, shaking a fist at them. To Joe's relief, Bevans made no move to go toward his own boat, which was tied to the bay side of the lighthouse base.

A dark wall of rain swept toward them. A long, crooked streak of lightning split the sky behind the lighthouse, turning it into a dark silhouette. The thunder came immediately, a blasting roar of sound.

Joe's pulse was thudding. "That was close!"

"The storm's closer!" Christy yelled. "Hang on! Here it comes!"

Joe stared in amazement. He could actually see the curtain of rain rushing at them. The Gulf surface beneath it churned into a white froth. Christy tossed him a life jacket. "If we tip over, hang on to Wishbone!"

Then the rain reached them, shocking and cold. Joe yelped as the stinging drops lashed him. Christy was yelling something.

"What?" Joe bellowed.

"Haul the starboard line! Quick!"

Joe grabbed it and pulled as hard as he could. The catamaran shuddered, changed course, and sped along, leaning dangerously.

"What now?" Joe asked urgently.

"I'm going to tie up at the pier! It's the closest thing around!" Christy yelled.

Getting there was tricky. The gray, lashing rain almost hid the shoreline. The choppy water threatened to overturn them at any moment. Christy had a steady hand with a boat, though. Joe admired her coolness as she steered with a sure instinct for safety.

"This will be tough," she warned. "I want you to climb up on the pier and tie us up. Don't fall in!"

"I'll try not to!"

They had to yell to hear each other. The rain was a loud roar, drumming on the fabric of the sail and banging on the aluminum pontoons. Joe crouched, getting ready. He scrambled out with a line in his hand, teetered for a second, then found his footing.

Before long, he had tied the catamaran to the pier. He quickly helped Christy and a soaked Cap'n Ahab ashore. The cat didn't seem to mind the soaking, unlike every other cat Joe had ever known. Then Joe pulled Wishbone to safety.

"This is awful," Christy said, holding up a hand to keep the blowing rain out of her eyes. "I think we're closest to the Gilmore place."

"Let's go!" Joe turned and began to trot along the dunes, with Wishbone right beside him.

Christy caught up with Joe and grabbed his arm. "No use running! We're as wet as we're going to get!" She looked back. "Come on, Cap'n Ahab!" The cat ran to join them.

The group slogged through the downpour, flinching at claps of thunder and bursts of lightning. After what to Joe seemed like hours, they came out in the backyard of the Gilmore house.

Carperdale met them at the door, tut-tutting. He hurried the dripping Christy into the downstairs bathroom and gave her a big towel and a thick blue terry-cloth robe. He took Joe into his own cozy apartment, bundled him into the bathroom there, and in a few moments brought him dry clothes from upstairs.

Joe came out, dressed, but with damp hair, and asked, "What did Mom say?"

"Why, nothing, Joseph."

Joe let out a sigh of relief. "You didn't tell her that we went out in this weather?"

"No," Carperdale said slowly. "That is hardly my place, Joseph. You must tell her, of course."

With a grimace, Joe said, "Yes, I guess I have to."

He dried Wishbone with a towel and noticed Cap'n Ahab in a corner, licking his wet fur.

He looked around. Carperdale's navy background showed plainly in the neat, efficient way the room was organized and decorated. An old photograph on one wall showed a much younger Carperdale dressed in a smart white uniform, standing on the deck of a large ship. Another showed Carperdale and a skinny man with the unmistakable Gilmore features posing beside a big fish. The only other photo was of a young Carperdale dressed in a tuxedo and standing beside a pretty woman wearing a bridal gown.

"My wife," Carperdale explained in a soft voice. "She passed away many years ago."

"I'm sorry," Joe said.

115

"Thank you. And I am sorry that your father passed away, Joseph."

"Thanks." Joe thought that Carperdale would have been his choice for an adopted grandfather. Somehow he knew that his dad would have liked the old man, too. He felt a little embarrassed and said, "Thanks for bringing me dry clothes, too. Is there anything Christy can wear?"

"She has borrowed one of Miss Rhonda's robes. I can rinse her clothes and have them dry in less than an hour. Right now Miss Christy is calling her grandmother to let her know she is safe here."

Wishbone had quietly left. Joe went to find him. The Jack Russell terrier was in the kitchen, gobbling dry food as fast as he could. With a chuckle, Joe said, "I didn't know you were so hungry, boy."

Wishbone barely looked up. He glared for a moment at Cap'n Ahab, who had followed Joe into the kitchen. Then he continued to polish off his well-earned meal.

Suddenly, a tremendous crash of thunder made the house shake. Ellen came downstairs looking for Joe. "There you are," she said. "I was worried that you were out in this mess."

Joe swallowed. Behind his mother he could see Carperdale, standing silently in the hall. "I sort of was out in it, Mom," Joe said quietly. He saw Carperdale give him a reassuring nod.

"He was with me, Mrs. Talbot." Ellen turned as Christy came in, bundled up in a dark blue robe much too large for her. "We were out on my catamaran when it started to rain. We came straight back here."

"Well," Ellen said doubtfully, "I suppose it's all right, since you're safe. Next time, be sure to check the weather report first."

"We will," Joe promised. "Mom, is Rhonda around?"

"She and Wanda are in the study, I think," Ellen replied.

"I've got something to ask her," Joe said.

Wanda and her cousin were sitting at the table in the study. Wanda still looked dejected. "Hi," Rhonda said when Joe, Christy, and Ellen came in. "Heavens, Christy, what happened to you?"

"We got caught in the rain," Christy said. "Carperdale's drying my clothes now."

Cap'n Ahab came padding into the room. Carperdale had towel-dried him. However, the orange cat looked a couple of sizes smaller, all the same. His damp fur clung close to his body. He glanced around the room, found a small oval rug, and curled up on it. In a moment, he was purring.

"That cat looks wet," Wanda said.

"He's used to it," Christy explained. "He even goes swimming in the Gulf sometimes."

Ellen laughed. "A very unusual cat."

Joe cleared his throat. "Miss Gilmore, I have something to ask you about the bay."

Rhonda seemed surprised by Joe's serious tone. "Yes?"

"Where's Charity?" Joe asked.

With a puzzled frown, Rhonda said, "Charity? Who's that?"

"Not a person. An island," Joe explained.

Rhonda looked at him blankly. "I never heard of it. There's a Faith Island and a Hope Island, but—"

Joe's copy of the poem had turned into a soaked mess. Rhonda had left Hugo's notebook on a shelf. Joe got it, found the copy of the poem, and pointed to a line. "See here? The poem talks about three sisters.

117

That must be Faith, Hope, and Charity, but there's no Charity. What happened to it?"

"I don't know," Rhonda said, a puzzled look on her face.

Wishbone came into the study just then, licking his chops. He sat down and stared at the sleeping cat. Joe leaned over to scratch his pal's ears.

"Well," Joe said, "in the Sherlock Holmes story 'The Musgrave Ritual,' nobody could find the treasure because the landscape had changed over the years. The house had been built up, and even the old trees in the garden were no longer the way they were hundreds of years earlier. Everything looked different. What if that's happened here, too?"

"An island disappearing?" Wanda asked. "I never heard of such a thing."

"It happens, though," Rhonda said thoughtfully. "Skeleton Reef itself is much smaller than it was two hundred years ago. Erosion can slowly wear one island away, and sea currents can pile up sand and build other islands. I don't know anything about a third island, though."

"Well," Christy said thoughtfully, "is there anywhere we could find old maps of the bay? Or do you know someone who is familiar with a lot of the history of the town?"

Rhonda looked uncomfortable. "The only person I can think of who might have old maps and who knows tons of stuff about the town's past isn't someone you'd want to talk to."

"Who is it?" Joe asked. "Maybe we've been looking at things the wrong way all along. Maybe if we just change the way we're thinking about the puzzle, the way Sherlock Holmes did in the story, everything would become clear."

Rhonda shook her head. "Joe, I know you mean

well, but really there's nothing to that old poem. Hundreds of people have looked for that treasure, but no one has ever found a trace of it." As if to underscore her words, thunder exploded, rattling the windows. The rain beat against the windows even harder than before, setting up a rushing roar.

"There's a chance, though, isn't there?" Christy asked. "Even if it's just a small one?"

Ellen said, "I suppose there's always a possibility."

"It isn't one you'll like, though," Rhonda said. "All right. I'll tell you the one person you could ask about old maps and vanished islands. I'm afraid, though, that the news won't do you any good at all. It's someone you already met, Joe."

"Who?" Joe asked eagerly.

He felt his stomach drop when Rhonda answered: "His name is Nathaniel Bevans, Joe, and you met him the other morning at Skeleton Reef Light."

Chapter Twelve

Joe and Christy sat on the porch of Gilmore's Rest, watching the storm. It gradually blew itself out. As the wind dropped, the air felt wonderful to Joe, cool and clean. Unfortunately, his spirits did not improve along with the weather. Carperdale called Christy to the door and handed over her freshly dried clothes. "You may freshen up in the bathroom, Miss Christy," he said.

After she had gone, Carperdale came out and looked at the sky. "Bracing weather," he commented. "When I was in the navy, I always enjoyed a good storm—especially when it ended!"

Joe nodded. "Carperdale, you said that you knew Nathaniel Bevans, right?"

Carperdale turned his bright gaze on Joe and stroked his moustache. "Indeed, I did, Joseph. What about him?"

Joe struggled to say it right. "Well . . . is he . . . dangerous?"

Carperdale considered the question. "No," he said at last. "I should say he is grumpy and irritable, but he'd never actually harm anyone physically."

"Then if I needed to ask him a question, would he answer it?"

With a shrug, Carperdale said, "Who knows, Joseph? I should think if you asked in the right way, and at just the right time, he might. I'll tell you something about Mr. Bevans. He loves that old lighthouse. He actually worries about people visiting it and getting hurt. I believe he sees himself as a kind of safety guard, actually. Perhaps if one appealed to his special fondness for the lighthouse, one could strike up a friendship with him."

"Thanks," Joe said.

"Don't mention it," returned Carperdale, and he went back inside.

Joe looked at Wishbone, who was stretched out on the porch. "Well, boy, I guess we have to go and visit him."

When Christy came outside a few minutes later, Joe told her his plan. She objected, but she could not think of anything better. So the two of them put Wishbone into the basket of the tandem bike and set off for Mr. Bevans's house, on Bay Street. Christy knew the way, so she steered. Cap'n Ahab, riding in her backpack, stared back at Joe.

Bay Street was in a quiet section of town. There were cracked sidewalks, bare yards overgrown with prickly little sand spurs and tough saw grass, and houses that looked battered by years of sun and rain. Most of the homes on the street stood twelve to fifteen feet off the ground, on stilts. Christy explained how the Gulf sometimes flooded this part of town during storms. The stilts kept the houses above the water and prevented severe storm damage.

Mr. Bevans's house was really only a small cottage, though it seemed larger because its stilts lifted it twelve feet off the ground. A set of wooden stairs ran up to a front deck. On the concrete pad beneath the house, a battered, rusty old Ford pickup truck was parked. Its black hood was still beaded with raindrops.

"Well," Christy said, staring at the place, "here we are, but I don't like it."

Joe nodded. "I don't like it, either, but I don't think we have any other choice. Do you think he's at home?"

"He must be." Christy pointed toward the truck. She turned in at the driveway and stopped the bike.

Joe climbed off. "Well, here goes."

Wishbone jumped down from the basket as Christy parked the bike. Then she let Cap'n Ahab out of her backpack. The cat looked around, acted bored, and started to lick himself. Wishbone seemed to make an effort to ignore the feline.

Feeling a fluttering in his stomach, Joe climbed up the steps leading to the front deck of the little house. Then he knocked on the old wooden door. Footsteps sounded from inside, and a moment later the door opened.

Mr. Bevans, his gray hair bristling, stood there staring at Joe and Christy. "What do ye want?" he growled.

"We want to talk to you about the lighthouse," Joe said, trying to control his voice. "We—"

"Ye had no business there!"

Joe lowered his gaze. "No, sir. You're right."

"It's a dangerous place. Old and tumbling down. Ye could have been hurt!"

"Yes, sir."

Christy spoke up. "If it's so dangerous, why do you go out there all the time?"

The old man frowned. "That's none of your

business, young lady! Ain't it enough that the doom of the lighthouse is on me? Can't ye young folks leave it alone?"

"Please," Joe said. "We need to talk to you."

"Go away!"

Joe started to say something, but at that moment Wishbone dived past him and sped through the open door. Mr. Bevans roared.

"He won't hurt anything!" Joe said. "Wishbone, come here!"

Mr. Bevans swung the door open. "Come in an' get him. Then get away from here."

The living room was surprisingly neat, with everything stored away. The furnishings were threadbare but clean. Wishbone peeked at Joe from one end of the sofa.

"There he is," Joe said. "I'm sorry. We know how much you like the lighthouse, and we just wanted—"

"You think you know that, eh?" Mr. Bevans rumbled. "That lighthouse has been bad luck to my whole family!"

Christy softly asked, "Wouldn't you like to tell us about it?"

Mr. Bevans seemed undecided. He looked at them suspiciously. "What would ye want to know? Long as you're in here, ye might as well sit down. Tell me what ye want, and be quick!"

Joe and Christy sat on the sofa, while Mr. Bevans sank into a beat-up old armchair. Wishbone lay on his stomach, observing the scene.

Joe began, "There's an old poem—"

"There!" roared Bevans. "I knew it! The two of ye are just like all the others—crazy for gold, crazy for treasure. Well, ye won't find Ben Walker's treasure. Ye'll find only heartbreak and hurt, I tell ye. Blast it

123

all, don't my family know? Ain't they suffered enough?"

"Please," Joe said, "just listen to us."

Meanwhile, Wishbone was taking in everything around him. *Hmm,* he thought, *everything's shipshape. There's a picture on the wall of a big ship in Hong Kong harbor. The coffee table is made of a round piece of glass sitting on top of an old ship's wheel. It's obvious that Mr. Bevans used to be a sailor! Sherlock Holmes would see that at once. Only, he might be a little more persuasive than Joe.*

Joe was getting nowhere. Mr. Bevans, sounding grumpier and grouchier by the minute, refused even to listen to him. Wishbone sensed that in a moment the old man would order Joe and Christy out of his house.

That was when his nose began to twitch. Without anyone noticing him, Wishbone rose and padded around to one end of the sofa. One item was out of place in the room—an old, worn catnip mouse. It was jammed between the back of the sofa and the wall. From the smell, it might have been there for months.

Wishbone sniffed again. *Odd,* he thought. *No cat has been around here for ages, but there's a cat toy.* Then he realized what must have happened. Like Sherlock Holmes, Wishbone made a connection—and he saw a way that might help Joe persuade this grouchy old man to cooperate.

Wishbone discovered that the front door was not completely closed. He scratched at it until it opened. Then he darted outside and down the steps. Cap'n Ahab's scent was plain enough. He was using one of the pilings that supported the house as a scratching post. Wishbone trotted right up to him. "Hey, Cap'n Ahab! Come with me."

The cat gave him a blank yellow-eyed stare.

"Come on! Christy needs you! Joe needs you! Follow me."

Cap'n Ahab yawned, showing his teeth.

Wishbone groaned. How in the world did a self-respecting dog deal with such an infuriating animal? He came closer to his orange adversary. "Look, you don't have to like me, and I don't have to like you. Still, we can come to an agreement. I need your help. Joe needs it. Christy needs it. Follow me, and you can eat out of my bowl any time you want."

The cat scratched himself with his hind foot, concentrating on the side of his head near his eye patch.

Wishbone snorted. "I'm going to help Joe. You stay here if you want. No dog would treat his best friend in the whole world the way you're treating Christy!"

Wishbone turned away and raced back up the steps. At the top, he turned around. Cap'n Ahab was still right where he had been when Wishbone had read him the riot act. *Doggone it,* he thought. *How can I get him inside?* He could run and bark at Cap'n Ahab, but the cat that ignored alligators probably wouldn't pay much attention to a Jack Russell terrier.

What would Sherlock Holmes do? Wishbone wondered. Then it hit him. *Why, he'd think like a cat! Let's see: Cats are curious, and they like to chase things, and they like . . . catnip!* He darted back inside the house.

Mr. Bevans was still upset. Christy and Joe had stood up, edging toward the door. Wishbone went straight to the sofa, hooked his teeth on the catnip mouse—*Yuk!* he thought. *Cat lips have touched this!*—and pulled it loose. He dashed outside and down the

125

steps. "Here, cat, take a sniff of this!" With a toss of his head, Wishbone threw the cat toy at Cap'n Ahab.

The big orange cat watched it land, then sniffed it. He started to purr.

Okay, Wishbone thought, *now for the tricky part!* He zipped in close, grabbed the catnip mouse right from under Cap'n Ahab's nose, then ran back up the steps. This time Cap'n Ahab followed him—fast, and with murder in his one good eye!

Wishbone flew through the door. "Yef! Thaf right! Now *catch!*" With a flip of his head, he tossed the toy to the cat.

The orange cat caught it in one paw and batted the catnip mouse across the floor. He went bounding after it and ran right across Mr. Bevans's foot. The man looked down, surprised, and stopped bellowing.

Wishbone was grinning. "Yes! Yes!" He licked his

lips. "Ugh! I'll taste catnip for a month! And I've completely lost my doggy dignity—but my guess was right. Mr. Bevans has a soft spot for cats!"

Cap'n Ahab had given up on the chase and was rubbing against Mr. Bevans's leg, purring loudly. Mr. Bevans bent over, reached his hand out, and tickled the top of the cat's head. Cap'n Ahab rumbled with delight.

Mr. Bevans sniffed. "That's a good-looking cat," he mumbled.

"His name's Cap'n Ahab," Christy said.

Mr. Bevans sat back in his chair, and Cap'n Ahab jumped up in his lap. "He reminds me of ol' Sailor," Mr. Bevans said in a gruff voice, stroking Cap'n Ahab's head. "Just an old alley cat that took up with me, but he lived here for fifteen years. Best friend I ever had. I sure missed him after he passed away." He pulled out a handkerchief and blew his nose.

"Cap'n Ahab's my best friend," Christy said softly.

Mr. Bevans nodded, running his fingers through Cap'n Ahab's fur just behind his head. "Everybody needs one, I reckon."

Wishbone felt a glow of pride. "How about that! Instant nice guy! That was a great idea, if I do say so myself. No wonder people think Mr. Bevans is odd. Anybody who'd lose his head over a cat has to be a little off."

Chapter Thirteen

r. Bevans coughed and looked up. "What did you
need, young folks? I'm sorry I blew up at ye." He
shook his head. "My family's been cursed by that lighthouse so long, I reckon it got to me."

Joe sensed that his chance had come. "Mr. Bevans,"
he said, "you're the only one in town who can tell us
this: There's a Faith Island and a Hope Island, but has
there ever been a Charity Island?"

Mr. Bevans frowned as he petted the cat. "Maybe.
Lot o' things changed along this stretch o' coast after
the big hurricane of 1837. River changed course. Half
the town washed away."

"Is there any way of telling for sure?" Christy
asked.

"Oh, aye. Come with me." Mr. Bevans pushed
himself up from the chair and led the way to a sort of
pantry. He opened it, revealing shelves crammed with
dusty old papers. Joe's nose started to itch. "Charts,"
Mr. Bevans said. "Maps an' charts datin' back to the
years when my ancestors kept the Skeleton Reef
Light—back to the disgrace of our family."

"What disgrace?" Joe asked.

As Mr. Bevans began to rummage through the folded maps, he sighed. "Ah, young feller, 'tis a bitter tale. Back in the days of old Ben Walker, a Bevans was the lighthouse keeper. The story goes that Walker wrecked his craft because my ancestor was drunk on duty. Drunk on duty! That was a swingin' offense in the navy back then—a noose around the neck, and haul 'im up to the yardarm! 'Tis the most shameful blot on the record ye could have."

"He let the light go out," Christy said, "because he was drunk?"

Mr. Bevans blew his nose again. "No," he said quietly. "'Tis worse. We in the family know it. 'Tis a tale told by father to son over all these years. That pirate Walker bribed Anthony Bevans, he did—paid him to put the light out that night. He was hopin' to lead to disaster two British ships that were huntin' him. One of 'em did ground itself on the reef. T'other, though, the HMS *Dolphin,* under the command o' Captain Patrick O'Brien, hauled off just in time. Walker seen the game was up, got his crew off in the boats, an' scuttled his ship, *Mad Mary's Revenge.*

"Then my ancestor took 'im into the lighthouse and hid 'im for three days. He tried to row ashore after that, but Captain O'Brien picked 'im up in the bay and jailed 'im. He died before goin' to trial, five or six weeks later on. Still, he left the clues carved into his bed, they say."

"Clues to a buried treasure," Joe said.

Bevans shook his head and pulled from a shelf a long, rolled-up sheet of paper, brittle and flaking. "Not to any buried treasure, son—to the place where he'd scuttled his ship. No one could locate it. Any treasure that Walker had was still in the hold o' the *Revenge,* though he let people believe his men had carried it all

129

away. See, he hoped to escape someday, and he knowed he'd need the bearin's. But the poem flat makes no sense. . . . Here we are. Come over to the table."

Carefully, Bevans unrolled the chart he'd taken from the pantry and placed it flat on a nearby table. A spicy, dusty odor rose from the brown, brittle old paper. It was a map of the bay, drawn on a large scale. Perhaps the ink had once been black, but it had faded to a chocolate color. The penmanship was fancy and detailed, with soundings—the depth of the water in different places—landmarks, and compass directions all laid out neatly. In old-fashioned handwriting, one corner of the map read: A CHART OF THE BAY OF ST. GEORGE, SHOWING THE PRINCIPAL CHANNELS, ETC. Below that was the date of 1809.

"Here is the lighthouse," Mr. Bevans said, touching an oval-shaped island.

Looking over the elderly man's shoulder, Joe saw that the lighthouse was actually marked on the map, together with a tiny square labeled KEEPER'S HOUSE, and another labeled FUEL HOUSE.

Joe studied the chart. "There *are* three islands!" he said, his voice excited. "Faith, Hope, and Charity!"

"The Sisters," Christy said, reading the spidery handwriting near the islands. "Only this isn't right. That island isn't Charity, it's Hope."

"What?" Bevans asked, leaning close. "Why, so it is! Look at that, would ye! Wait a minute!" He hurried away.

Wishbone was leaping up, trying to see what was on the table. Joe pushed him gently back down. "Sit, boy." To Christy, Joe said, "I don't understand. The islands have changed?"

"Look," Christy said, pointing at the western island. "This is Faith on the map, and this is where Faith Island still is—only it isn't this large anymore. I guess the hurricane must have washed about a third of it away." She moved her finger to the middle island. "This small one, closest to the shore, is labeled Hope. And the eastern one is Charity. Except today, the eastern one is Hope."

"Here we are." Mr. Bevans had brought over another pair of maps. He unrolled one on the floor. "Now, this one was made in 1843, six years after the big hurricane. Look at this." He pointed to the map, showing Joe and Christy that the only two islands were Faith and Charity—except that Charity was now called Hope.

"Oh, wow!" Christy said. "I think I see what happened. No one could find the spot where the treasure was supposed to be, because everything changed— even the names!"

"This is a modern-day navigational chart," Mr. Bevans said, unrolling the third map. "Let's compare it with the one from 1809."

With ruler and pencils, Joe and Christy did some quick calculations. "I was right," Joe said, comparing the two maps. "The hurricane changed everything.

131

The storm must have choked up the old river channel with sand, so the river moved about a half mile to the west. Sand collected between the old Hope Island and the mainland, until it wasn't really an island anymore. Then the river must have dropped silt, sort of gluing the old Hope Island into the mainland. And people who remembered that the eastern island was Hope started to call the old Charity Island by the wrong name—Hope Island."

"Confusing," Mr. Bevans said. "It must have happened that way, though. An' folks was slow to come back an' settle the town after the big blow. That's probably why nobody noticed they was callin' the island by the wrong name."

"Here," Christy said, drawing an *X* on the modern-day map. "Charity Island ought to be this hill, and right at the south point of it is where the pirate ship sank."

Mr. Bevans blinked. "If it's there, an' if we can find it, then it will sort of make up for my family's disgrace, won't it?"

"Sure it will," Christy said.

Cap'n Ahab came over and rubbed against Mr. Bevans's hand.

"All right," Mr. Bevans said, petting the cat, his face lighting up with excitement. "What are we waiting for? Let's go find the wreck o' the *Mad Mary's Revenge!*"

Chapter Fourteen

Mr. Bevans drove Joe and Wishbone back to Rhonda's house in his truck. Christy and Cap'n Ahab followed on the tandem bike. On the porch of Gilmore's Rest, Wanda listened to Joe's story. Her eyes grew wide. She yelled for Ellen, Rhonda, and Carperdale, and before fifteen minutes had passed, they organized themselves into a treasure-hunting party. They drove to the Municipal Gardens in Mr. Bevans's truck and the Rolls-Royce.

"I don't know about this," Rhonda said as they got out. She, Ellen, Wanda, Joe, Christy, and Carperdale stood next to the Rolls-Royce, which was parked behind Mr. Bevans's old pickup. Then Rhonda grabbed a shovel. "But we may as well see what's there! After all, these are the Municipal Gardens—they belong to everyone in town!"

"I brought this," Mr. Bevans said, holding up a six-foot-long iron rod. "I thought I could push it down into the soil, see if there's anythin' solid—"

"Quite a good idea, Mr. Bevans," Carperdale said with a smile. "However, if you will permit me, I think I have something that might be faster." He opened the trunk of the Rolls and took out a device that looked a little like a weed trimmer. "This is a metal detector," he explained. "Finding old coins on the beach is one of my hobbies."

Joe grinned. This was really detecting! He couldn't help thinking that if Sherlock Holmes had been able to use modern technology, no crook would ever have gone free.

Carperdale put a pair of headphones on. Joe and Christy walked beside him as he moved the detector around the roses, the pansies, the azaleas, and all the other flowers. Wishbone was sniffing like crazy. That made Joe wonder exactly what a 250-year-old ship might smell like!

Forty minutes after Carperdale had started working, he stopped, his eyes gleaming. "Something very large is here," he said. "And it's not too terribly far beneath the surface. Mr. Bevans, pass me a shovel!"

Before anyone could make another move, Wishbone was already at it, digging furiously. By the time they had the three shovels out, Wishbone was in a hole almost as deep as he was tall. Joe had to move him out of the way before anyone else was able to start digging.

Mr. Bevans, Carperdale, and Joe shoveled away in the middle of a sandy path. They were careful not to disturb the flowerbeds. Wishbone came back to the edge of the hole and began to dig, too. He burrowed down with all the energy he had. Joe noticed that Cap'n Ahab, as usual, was lying in the sun and staring. Well, that was all right. After all, the Cap'n had done his part!

The hole got deeper. Passersby looked at them curiously, but no one stopped to ask what was going on. Rhonda said that was because the shovelers seemed to know what they were doing. Finally, when Mr. Bevans and Carperdale were standing in a hole deeper than their waists, Mr. Bevans's shovel struck wood.

"Careful," Carperdale said. He went to the Rolls and brought back a garden trowel. With very cautious strokes, he gently scraped dirt away from the rotten old planks. The trowel clinked against metal. "What's this?" He scraped more soil away.

Joe blinked down at something that looked like a big red doughnut. What in the world could it be? "Is that rusty iron?" he asked.

"It is," Carperdale murmured. He looked up. "This is the mouth of a cannon! The remainder of the gun is underneath, straight up and down. The ship must be resting on its side."

"Aye," Bevans said, his eyes glistening. "An' if there's gold aboard her, we'll have it in another hour!"

"Uh . . . excuse me," Wanda said. Everyone looked at her. She bit her lip. "This is wonderful, and I love history, and it might really, really help to find gold—but we can't dig anymore."

"We can't?" Joe asked, sounding astonished.

"No," Wanda said firmly. "If this is actually a ship from 1765, then it has to be excavated by archeologists. They are professionals who know what they're doing."

Carperdale clapped Mr. Bevans on the shoulder. "Miss Wanda is right, you know."

"Aye," said Mr. Bevans. He sighed. "At least promise me that ye'll let 'em know I helped. I want people to understand that not all the Bevans family is undependable."

"You're very dependable," Christy said. "My cat likes you, and he's never wrong about anyone."

Cap'n Ahab looked at them both from his single

yellow eye. No one could interpret his expression. At least Joe couldn't.

Joe's head began to spin before the day was over. Wanda had made a long-distance phone call to an archeologist named Dr. Harrison at Oakdale College. He had promised to make a trip out to the site as soon as possible. He would bring a whole team, he said.

Next the newspaper reporters came. They asked Joe and Christy question after question. Two radio reporters showed up in a van, and they interviewed Joe, Christy, and Mr. Bevans.

The next day, Dr. Harrison and his crew arrived. The St. George Bay city council, aware of the fantastic publicity the town was getting, gave him permission to excavate the ship. After a few hours of work, Dr. Harrison announced that yes, indeed, the ship did appear to be a vessel from the year 1765 or a little earlier. They had definitely found the *Mad Mary's Revenge*.

That day the TV crews showed up. Joe and Christy were interviewed, Joe holding Wishbone and Christy holding Cap'n Ahab. Wanda was interviewed, and she explained all about the lighthouse. Mr. Bevans, beaming and no longer looking grumpy at all, told of his long struggle to restore his family's good name. He thanked Joe and Christy—and especially Cap'n Ahab.

The local TV story appeared on the national news. By the weekend, donations were pouring in from all around the country. When it became obvious that enough funds would be collected to save the lighthouse, Wanda announced that the Oakdale Historical Society would allow the St. George Lighthouse Preservation Society to take the responsibility of doing the repairs.

Mr. West and Mrs. Xavier, both smiling from ear to ear, agreed at once. They were videotaped by a news team as they displayed a huge pile of checks and pledges for more donations that had already come in.

Wanda took Joe and Christy aside. "You did it!" she said. "The city is already planning to re-name the Municipal Gardens the Treasure Gardens. The site is going to be a historical landmark, and so is the lighthouse. There is even talk about appointing Mr. Bevans as the official caretaker!"

"I'm glad the lighthouse is going to be restored," Joe said.

"The bay wouldn't be the same without it," Christy added.

"And the Oakdale Historical Society won't be ruined after all!" Wanda said. "From now on, I'm going to think twice before accepting any gifts on behalf of the society! I've learned my lesson!"

Wishbone barked. Joe laughed. "I think he's happy for you."

Wanda smiled. "Well, I'm happy that for once his habit of digging really paid off!"

In Wishbone's opinion, the very best reward came a few days later. When Wanda, Ellen, Joe, and Wishbone went to the airport to check in for their flight home, everyone recognized them right away because of the TV coverage. As Joe was saying goodbye to Christy, Carperdale, Mr. Bevans, and Rhonda, the airline people were conferring, smiling, and pointing at Wishbone.

One of the employees said to Ellen, "We know about your son and his dog. They found the treasure ship! Well, as a sort of reward, we'd like to offer your party first-class tickets back to Oakdale. And Wishbone can ride with you, if he's well behaved."

Wishbone looked up proudly. "I'm *always* well behaved!"

And that was how, a few minutes later, Wishbone got to sit in Joe's lap as they took off. He gazed out the window as the plane climbed high into the blue sky. He grinned when he saw the town of St. George Bay spread out just like a wonderful three-D map.

"Ah, this is the way to travel! Here I am, right where I belong, next to my buddy, Joe! And we're zooming through the air! I'm a flying-ace dog!" Wishbone's nose twitched. "And best of all—yes, I smell it— best of all, here comes some of that great airline food I've heard so much about!"

About Brad Strickland

BRAD STRICKLAND is a writer and college professor who lives in the small town of Oakwood, Georgia. He likes the ocean, pirate tales, sailing, and lighthouses, and so he enjoyed having the chance to co-write *The Treasure of Skeleton Reef* with his friend Thomas E. Fuller. Inspired by the real lighthouse on St. George's Island off the coast of Florida, Brad created the imaginary town of St. George Bay. Just like the lighthouse in this book, the real St. George's Island lighthouse is in danger of being destroyed, and it has its very own Lighthouse Preservation Society. Brad hopes the group succeeds in saving the landmark!

In addition to creating this story, Brad has written *Be a Wolf!* and *Salty Dog*, two Wishbone Adventures. He has also written or co-written twenty-two other novels, fifteen of them for young readers. His first young-adult novel was *Dragon's Plunder*, a story of adventure on the high seas. He co-wrote four books with the late John Bellairs, and he continues to write books in Bellairs's popular young-adult mystery series, most recently *The Hand of the Necromancer*. With his wife, Barbara, Brad has co-written stories in the *Star Trek* and *Are You Afraid of the Dark?* novel series. He and Thomas Fuller have worked together on radio plays, short stories, and other writing projects.

Brad and Barbara have two children, Jonathan and Amy. In addition to teaching and writing, Brad enjoys photography, travel, and amateur acting. He and his wife have numerous pets, including cats, ferrets, a rabbit, and two dogs, neither of whom has ever found a treasure.